#3
6.97
WP

The Nightmare Candidate

The Nightmare Candidate

Ramona Stewart

DELACORTE PRESS/NEW YORK

Published by
Delacorte Press
1 Dag Hammarskjold Plaza
New York, N.Y. 10017

Manufactured in the United States of America

First printing

Typography by Jack Ellis

Library of Congress Cataloging in Publication Data

Stewart, Ramona, 1922–
The nightmare candidate.

I. Title.
PZ3.S85196Ni   [PS3569.T468]   813'.54   80-365
ISBN 0-440-06135-0

To Cynthia Vartan

"That which hath been is now;
and that which is to be hath already been."

Eccles. 3:15

PART ONE

Chapter 1

On her nineteenth birthday Elissa Blake woke in the middle of the night. Her eyes flew open and she lay listening to the man beside her as if her waking might break the filmstrip of his dream. When his breathing remained steady, she tried to make out the sounds of New York City, which were still new enough to her to be exotic—the siren scream above the hive drone of traffic, the subway rumble in the concrete below, garbage trucks clanking and grinding. But she was in a soundproof suite in the Museum of African Art. There were no windows and she heard nothing but the air conditioning. After a bit she sat up, her pale hair streaming down her naked breasts. Then she rose to stand clear of the bed.

In the shadowed room her hair shone like phosphorescence, cresting above the finely molded forehead and swirling down her shoulders and her straight young spine. But the rest of her was blurred by darkness, and though her foot touched her crumpled slacks and sweater, she lingered, gazing at the man on the bed.

At thirty-five he still had an athlete's well-muscled

chest. By leaning intently toward him she could make out the hawklike features that still surprised her when they confronted her from the presidential primary billboards. He was Governor now and would by November probably be President.

As if her gaze troubled his sleep, he flung himself over on his pillow and she stepped back. She lingered, irresolute, then picked her way through the dark maze of unfamiliar furniture.

Switching on the bathroom light, she inspected the tow fluff between her long, slender legs. It had been her first time with a man but the bleeding had been light and it had already stopped. She ran the gilded dolphin taps of the wash basin and dried her fingers humbly on a corner of a thick towel. A raw silk robe hung on the back of the door, and on impulse she laid her cheek against it. Then she turned to her reflection in the medicine cabinet glass. But the sea-blue eyes regarded her unchanged. The delicate nose and pink lips still had a child's air. Though she bent closer, she could not see that the night had made a difference. Gravely considering, she turned away, looped her bright hair into a coil on the crown of her head, and stepped past the frosted door into the shower.

For a while she played with the water, sliding the spray lever back and forth and changing the flow to different temperatures. She sniffed the scented oval of soap through its rich wrapper but could not bring herself to tear the paper and completed her bath with clear water. It was when she turned off the tap that she heard the angry voices.

They were shouting in the bedroom. "Get the hell out," Cameron cried. Another man answered but his answer was incoherent. She froze, water still streaming from her. He was alone—she had left him sleeping. The suite was secret.

"For God's sake don't—" She couldn't tell which voice had risen in pain or terror.

"Jesus—" It was cut off by a volley of obscenity. The propelling rage shocked her more than the actual words. It was insane rage, freighted with murder.

A shot seemed to smash into the shower stall. Her body jerked as a second shot rang out. Then she stood, deafened, huddled into herself.

There was silence.

As the seconds coiled away, she strained to listen, but all she heard was her own bewildered whimper. "Steve?" she whispered. But no one in the next room could have heard.

She crept from the shower stall, realized she was naked, and, pulling a crimson towel from the rack, wound it into a sarong.

"Steve?" she called more loudly.

But still she heard nothing. As she listened at the bathroom door, the silence thickened.

"Please," she whispered to no one in particular. Her fingers touched the doorknob. She grasped it and slowly turned it to crack the door a few inches. Then she looked into the darkened bedroom.

There was no intruder, no sound, no movement. The room seemed unchanged. At first, she thought he was still sleeping. But as she opened the door wider, the bathroom light shafted across the bed.

He lay drowned in blood. Blood pooled on the well-muscled chest and soaked the blue satin sheet that still half covered him. And where his head had been—the handsome hawklike face, the penetrating blue eyes, the flashing Cameron smile—there was only a thing like a smashed melon.

She stood in the doorway like a mannequin, staring at the bloody chest, the puddled sheet, the exploded stump that had been Steve Cameron's head. She could hear the whir of an electric clock; her nostrils caught the sharp scent of vodka, the spicy scent of aftershave. Then the bathroom light caught a glitter in the headboard and she tiptoed closer. It was the glitter of a gold-filled tooth, torn from his jaw by some trick of explosion and embedded in the wood. She reached out to it. The slime of blood and brain tissue on her fingers cracked her, snapped off something in her consciousness. And as her naked foot touched her sweater on the rug, she began to move like an automaton.

Dropping the towel, she drew on her jeans and slowly zipped them. For a moment she stood as if she were trying to recall something very difficult. Then she crouched on her hands and knees and found her shoes and socks. Her pale hair loosened and tumbled down her shoulders as she pulled on her sweater, drew on her socks, and stepped into her loafers. A heartbroken cry escaped her. At the sound, she turned and walked to the bedroom door. "Steve," she repeated.

A white porcelain lamp lit the sitting room and she paused, focusing on a bowl of brilliant anemones. In the white room, surrounded by thick white carpet, white drapes against the whitewashed walls, the masses of red and purple wild flowers were brilliant. Her gaze detached itself and roamed to Cameron's coat, thrown on the sofa with her own parka beside it. She moved to her jacket and hooked a finger through its collar loop. Dragging the coat, she went to the bar and pressed the secret spring behind a crystal decanter. The wall slid open and she stepped into the darkness of the museum and began to move past the bronze Benin heads and Gelede cult masks, past ancestral screens and an iron god from Dahomey.

Beside an Ogiyen shrine she pressed the iron bar of a fire door. It was locked and for a moment she bent her head in a helpless movement. Then her fingers touched the latch and she slid the bolt. The door opened and the cold night air rushed at her.

As she went down the walk between the museum and the next office building, her loafers crunched the icy crust of a late February snowfall. She came out on the cross street, empty except for an occasional cruising taxi. But she didn't hail one. Still trailing her parka, she moved slowly through the night to Park Avenue, turned the corner, and headed south.

Chapter 2

Jenny Beck woke next morning in the old sleigh bed in her Greenwich Village apartment, reached for her glasses, and squinted at her wristwatch. Then she rolled over and shook Al Martin.

"Hey. You overslept."

He made an ambiguous noise and slid his head beneath his pillow. Jenny sat up and ran her fingers through her dark hair. She was small and bright-eyed, with a happy resemblance to a friendly squirrel. She shook her bedmate. "Get up. It's eight thirty." She waited, then snatched at his pillow, but he grabbed it. She tugged but finally had to give up. Victory established, he emerged, smiling benignly. He was already balding, with a wild fringe of black hair and warm, nearsighted brown eyes.

"I don't have a class till ten," he accused her.

"Don asked you to take his nine o'clock. Remember?"

"I hate these master-slave relationships."

"When you're a professor, you'll have your own teaching assistants."

He looked more cheerful. "I'll make them feel the lash."

"That's my darling. Now how about it? Up."

He also reached·for his glasses and consulted his watch. "Holy snakes," he said and shot out of bed. He was well over six feet and at twenty-six he still had the spare, rangy build of a basketball center. "Coffee," he croaked and shambled to the bathroom.

Jenny found her slippers rolled up in her pajama bottoms at the foot of the bed. She put them on, turned up the thermostat, and padded through the homey disorder of the living room into the kitchen. Removing Smythies' *Science and E.S.P.* and Vasiliev's *Experiments in Distant Influence* from the stove, she made coffee and took their mugs to the bathroom where Al, having shaved and showered, was toweling off.

He asked, "Was that Elissa who buzzed downstairs last night?"

"Yep. Must have left her key somewhere."

"Where had she been?"

"Don't know. There's a lot of static on that intercom."

"Too bad she missed her birthday party."

"Well, I should have told her we were having one."

He went to the bedroom, Jenny following with the mugs, while he threw on his clothes. "But where could she go?"

"She might have worked late. Taking pix at some banquet—Dockworkers United or the Radical Millionaires. Cameron's campaign is hotting up." He had been caught by surprise in New Hampshire but was expected to do well in Massachusetts.

"Come on. Till three in the morning?"

"More like four. Maybe Daddy Warbucks seduced her."

"You have a sick mind."

"I'm suspicious of rich politicians."

"He's known her since she was a child, for God's sakes."

"Mm. When will I see you?"

He went to the living room and threw books into his book bag. "I've got the statistics seminar at three. Then I have to stop at the library. Say six. How about you?"

"I'll be home right after work." She was an editorial assistant at a book publisher's.

"What'll we do this weekend? Wanna get married?"

"It's only been a couple of years. Let's get to know each other better."

"There's ice hockey at the Garden."

"How about the Telemann concert?" And when he groaned: "Baroque music makes me feel erotic."

"Okay, you're on."

When he left, Jenny poured herself another mug of coffee and made a desultory stab at tidying the stacks of manuscripts and books scattered around the living room. She tossed the pillows back on the chintz-covered sofa, straightened the hooked rugs, and pushed the cherrywood rocking chair back into place by the window. Then she went into the bedroom and made up the sleigh bed. But her mind kept returning to Elissa.

Since they'd known her, she had never come home so late, and Jenny and Al were the only people she knew in the city. Except for Steve Cameron. Jenny considered what she knew about Elissa.

She had knocked at their door one snowy January evening a month ago while Jenny was cooking dinner. Al had answered, and from the kitchen Jenny heard only murmurs until she came out to set the table. She was surprised to find a young blond stranger watching Al open their living room window.

"Meet Elissa," Al said. "She's going to use our fire escape to get in upstairs."

"Now wait a minute," said Jenny firmly.

The girl turned and Jenny saw that besides the startling long pale hair, she was very lovely. Thunder-blue eyes regarded her from some area of inner stillness. "You think I'm a burglar," she said in astonishment.

"Not necessarily," Jenny told her. "But you've got to admit it's an odd request."

The girl seemed to consider. She had an objective air, as if she could stand off and see herself without emotional involvement. After a moment the child-pink lips moved in a smile that lit up her face. "I guess I could be a burglar," she said. "But I really just left my key inside my apartment. My window's open and if I can go up your fire escape, I won't have to call a locksmith."

"The super's out and locksmiths get a mint after five o'clock," said Al, clearly taking the girl's side. Al was an optimist and recklessly trusting.

"My name's Blake," the girl said. "Maybe you've seen it downstairs on the mailbox." She reached in her shoulder bag for a wallet and produced a Florida state driver's license. "See, it even has my picture."

Jenny reached to the coffee table for her glasses and inspected the picture. It was in color and a good likeness. The address was a postbox in Key West. Elissa came around and watched over her shoulder.

"We live on a houseboat, so we have to use a postbox."

"We?" Jenny asked, knowing she was embarrassing Al, but the name Blake, together with Key West and a houseboat, touched a tab in her mind.

"My father and I."

"Is he Sam Blake?" Jenny asked and as Elissa nodded, the odd quality she'd sensed seemed more understandable.

She knew Sam Blake from his books. They had come out in the late 1950s and been the germinal work of the Beats, sending a generation off to Big Sur and the Haight. There had been only two of them, however. The third, in progress for ten years, had been slowed by attacks of writer's block. Also, Jenny had guessed from old magazine interviews, by periodic bouts with booze and drugs. A strange life for a girl, growing up on a houseboat in the tropics with an alcoholic writer. It would explain her difference from the usual run of lovely girls.

"I like his books," Jenny said, feeling a good deal less suspicious. "How come you're in New York? Going to school?"

"Only part-time. Mostly I'm a staff photographer for Steve Cameron's election headquarters."

"How's that for coincidence?" asked Al. "Did you know he owns this building? Of course, the family owns half of New York, so I guess it's not so surprising."

When Elissa nodded, Jenny felt there was something too quickly casual about the nod. It was as if she were hoping to block more questions. Jenny's curiosity flared.

"Do you actually know him?" she asked.

"Yes," Elissa said, and unaccountably her forehead flushed.

"Is that how you got past the waiting list? Did he help you get your apartment?"

"Hey, Jenny!" Al protested, "you're being downright nosy."

But Elissa was still young enough to feel she had to reply to questions. The ruddy blush spread from her forehead and stained her cheeks. "Yes," she said softly.

Why, the dirty old man, Jenny thought in outrage. Steve Cameron was only thirty-five, but this girl, this strange, gentle *child* was still a teen-ager.

"Is she cleared now to use our fire escape?" asked Al in a valiant try to hurry past the moment's embarrassment.

"What? Oh sure." Jenny handed back Elissa's driver's license.

Elissa threw it into her shoulder bag, smiled unsurely, and without another word ducked out their window. They heard her climb the metal fire stairs to her own apartment.

But Jenny learned she had been wrong in her leap to conclusions. When she and Al invited Elissa to dinner the next Sunday, they found that the entire Cameron family knew Elissa. The Camerons' winter fishing camp was near Key West, and they had all known her since she'd been a girl.

Still, Jenny decided, girls grow up. The unexpected can suddenly enter an old relationship. As she showered and dressed to go to work, Jenny tried to guess if anything was happening now between Elissa and Cameron. But except for her early shyness when his name came up, Elissa had never hinted there was more than a long friendship, and she seemed too candid for playacting. Her shyness when his name was first mentioned might have been shame at using influence to jump the waiting list for her apartment. As she ran a comb through her short dark hair, Jenny decided Al was probably right.

At nine o'clock she phoned Elissa so that she wouldn't be late for her job at campaign headquarters. But this morning there was no answer. It seemed odd. It wasn't likely she'd have risen and left for work early after getting home so late last night. On impulse she went upstairs and found Elissa sitting on the hall floor beside her door.

"Elissa."

She did not look up, did not seem to hear. Jenny bent over her and Elissa tilted a face that was disturbingly blank.

"Where's your key? You haven't been sitting here since you rang the downstairs buzzer?" She had, of course, Jenny realized. If she had lost her front door key, she'd probably lost her apartment key also. Jenny had been too sleepy at the time to realize it.

Jenny ran down the flight of stairs without waiting for the elevator. She crossed her own living room, catching up a bottle of vodka which might help with shock, and climbed the fire escape to Elissa's floor. Fortunately Elissa was still careless about locking her windows. She went through into Elissa's apartment and unlocked the door to the hall.

"Get up."

Elissa regarded her dazedly, and Jenny put a hand on her shoulder. "Let's go inside."

At Jenny's touch Elissa rose and allowed herself to be

guided into the bare little apartment. The furniture had been bought at the Salvation Army during one of her lunch hours: two wicker chairs, a standing lamp, a bureau, a coffee table, a low divan that served as a bed. Boxes of film were scattered on the coffee table. A Cameron poster was taped to one wall. At the sight of it Elissa made a despairing sound. "He's dead."

"Who?" And as Elissa went on staring at the poster, "Not Steve Cameron?"

Elissa sank to the divan and regarded her loafers, soaked through with melted ice and snow. Vaguely, she touched a slender finger to them.

My God, Jenny thought, it was possible. They hadn't turned on the news that morning. He could have been assassinated.

She went to the kitchen and poured vodka into a glass. Elissa resisted—she had a fear of alcohol because of her father—but Jenny managed to make her drink.

"How?" she asked. "Where did it happen?"

"The museum."

"What museum?"

"You know, their museum."

"The African Art?"

"In the secret suite."

In frustration Jenny picked up Elissa's little radio. She switched it on and was blasted by rockabilly music. She tried another station but got a morning talk show. Surely if Cameron had been assassinated . . .

"What secret suite, Elissa?"

The lovely brow moved with the difficulty of concentrating. "You push a spring behind a fetish."

"You went to this place with Cameron?"

Elissa nodded.

"My God," Jenny breathed. Secret suites with springs behind African fetishes. Al had far too trusting a nature.

Elissa moved as if Jenny had actually spoken. The blue eyes focused accusingly. "His father put it in when he built the museum. I think his father had a lady. Anyway, now the whole family uses it."

The vodka had thinned the shock and Jenny tried to press through to her quickly. "Tell me what happened. It's important, Elissa."

"It was my birthday."

"And Cameron found out?"

"He always remembers."

I'll bet he does, Jenny thought bitterly. From his secretary's tickler system; names and birthdays were a politician's stock in trade.

But she managed not to say it.

"He took me to dinner at the Nirvana. That's a restaurant overlooking Central Park with a view of the city lights—"

"I know where it is," Jenny said grimly. The full treatment, she thought; she felt like killing Cameron. Then she remembered somebody already had. "Wasn't it late to go to the museum?"

"He—Steve—wanted to give me a present. A water spirit."

"A what?"

"A little bronze figure. It was in a case. It's their museum, so that's all right. Wait, I'll show you." She looked about her, then shook her head. "No, it's in my purse. I left it."

At the memory she bent over, shivering. Jenny caught up the glass and made her drink again.

"Is that where it happened? He was killed in the museum?"

Elissa nodded, silent tears spilling down her face.

"Who killed him?"

"I don't know."

Jenny looked at her sharply as Elissa rocked back and forth.

"It wasn't you, Elissa, was it? You didn't kill him?"

Surprise straightened her. "Me? Kill Steve?"

"Tell me what happened."

"I came out of the bathroom—I heard a quarrel. And a shot. I guess two shots. I came out—" She made a painful try at breathing. "He was on the bed, all bloody."

"Maybe he wasn't dead. Did you call a doctor?"

She was sobbing now. Jenny put her arms around her. "His head was gone. One of his teeth—"

"Okay, baby, don't think about that part. Just tell me what happened. What did you do next?"

"I don't remember."

"But you're here. They let you go. What did the police—"

"No police." The voice was stifled against Jenny's chest. An awful suspicion snaked into Jenny's mind.

"You mean nobody knows? What about the Secret Service? Aren't they supposed to guard presidential candidates?"

"We got rid of them when we left the restaurant. Steve pretended to go to the men's room but he really went out the kitchen and we met again downstairs. It seemed like fun to be on our own for the evening."

"But how did you get into the museum? Isn't there a watchman?"

"Sure. He let us in. I mean, why not? The Camerons own the museum. He must have been making his rounds when I left."

"But didn't he hear something? If there were shots—"

"It's soundproof."

"You mean Cameron's just lying there? And the watchman saw you come in— Oh my God, your purse! Is that where you left it? In that crazy secret suite?"

"Yes."

"But Elissa, when they find it, they'll think you did it!"

The blue gaze told her the thought was monstrous.

"Where was the gun?"

"I didn't look for it. He was lying there—all blood."

"But you've got to call the police and report it. No,

wait, let me think. It's been so long now. Maybe Al should talk to somebody at the law school."

The phone rang, tearing the silence. When Elissa remained frozen, Jenny picked it up.

"Hello," she said tentatively. Then her face lost all expression. "Just a minute." She held the receiver toward Elissa. When Elissa moved back as if refusing, she said, "Take it!"

At her tone Elissa's fingers closed around the instrument. Her face still pled with Jenny as she slid the receiver beneath the bright hair. Then she straightened.

"Elissa? It's Steve."

Her lips parted. She tried to speak but no sound came out. Jenny rose and went to the window.

"What happened to you? When I woke, you were gone."

There was silence.

"You left your purse. Look—I just got back to my place. I've got to make the trip to Massachusetts. The car's waiting to take me to the airport. Jay can bring your purse down to headquarters. I'll call you later. Elissa!"

"Yes," she whispered.

"Is something wrong? You're not upset?" Silence. "Hell, here comes Jay. I can't talk now. I'll call you from Boston."

She nodded with her eyes closed. When he rang off, she slowly hung up.

Jenny turned from the window. "That was Cameron."

Elissa nodded.

"So he isn't dead."

"He didn't know that anything happened."

Jenny was silent.

"His head was shattered. I saw it." Her face lifted in bewilderment.

"It might have been some trick of light. Or your imagination."

"No."

"Had you fallen asleep? Maybe you just dreamed it."

"I didn't dream it."

"What was it then?"

She shook her head and the long shining hair swung loosely.

"Why didn't you tell him?"

But at that, the sea-blue eyes darkened, the childlike face closed.

"Leave me alone," she said.

Chapter 3

When Jenny left, Elissa walked to the window and stared out at the old chimney pots that sprang like mushrooms from the neighboring rooftops. Suddenly she turned and went to the phone to call Sam Blake. But she let her hand fall from the instrument. Instead, she sank into a wicker chair and gazed at the wall poster of Steve Cameron.

They had met when she was twelve, one day when she was scavenging the mangroves around the deserted islands in the Gulf off Key West. She had been doing that a lot then. It was tricky asking friends home to the houseboat with Sam drinking and brooding about his unfinished novel, so after school she mostly hung about by herself. Usually she took out Sam's battered, flat-bottomed skiff that he tied up to the stern of their houseboat. Sometimes she dove the reefs for conch and lobster. But sometimes she picked up old bottles after storms and high tides on the mangrove-tangled islands. Lately she'd found some fairly rare ones—a blue Key West Coca-Cola bottle and an amber rum bottle marked Santiago, Cuba, that Sam said might actually be worth saving. She'd got a book on antique bottles from the library and was starting to make a real collection.

On this afternoon she was running in close to where she'd found the Coca-Cola bottle, keeping a sharp eye on the mangrove roots, when she saw the red Mako.

It was the kind of rig she and Sam could only dream of: twenty-one foot with twin 200 Evinrude outboards, its chrome blazing away in the tropic sunlight. And nobody was in it. She supposed its owner had gone up on the island—it was one of the keys that had formed a patch of sand and had grown a few sea oats and wild grasses. She knew she shouldn't go up to a boat in its owner's absence, but it was too new and beautiful to resist. She cut her motor and let the current carry her skiff closer. When she arrived at its stern, she held herself off with one hand on an engine while she gazed with admiration at the dive platform mounted on the stern and the red upholstered swivel chairs. It was a moment before she noticed the props and lower units on both engines. She caught her breath at such damage to two powerful new engines and she was still staring at them in dismay when a man came around a path through the mangroves and hailed her.

"Hey!" he shouted. "I need your help! I'm stranded."

She watched in silence as he came down the little beach and approached her. He was tall and tanned and well muscled in abbreviated trunks. He was about twenty-eight, one of those handsome, golden men the keys produce in such profusion that she didn't notice anything unusual. But as he waded into the clear water and came closer, she was struck by the mobility of his hawklike features and the quickness of his piercing blue eyes. She noticed, too, his disappointment when he saw her age and cast a swift glance at the dilapidated skiff in which she was standing.

"Hi," he said in a friendly tone that despaired of her being any help to him.

But she stood her ground under the assault to her pride. "What wiped you out?"

He seemed marginally encouraged by her having noticed his engines. "Coral head. I missed the channel."

"You must have really been flying."

"It's badly marked."

She nodded. "You've got to read the water."

"The sun went under the clouds for a second."

She nodded again and they stood in more comradely silence, brooding down at the props and the damaged engines.

At last he said, "Do you suppose you could run me to shore to make a phone call?"

"And leave your boat here unattended?" she asked, unable to mask her disapproval.

"Well," he said, admitting the recklessness of his policy. Neither of them spoke of his reluctance to wait on a deserted key, trusting a twelve-year-old to make the phone call. And he was too kind to mention that an adult rescuer could have taken him in tow.

She sighed. "What marina do you want?"

He considered her thoughtfully, shot a somber look at the skiff.

"I can make it. Don't worry," she said. "We can rig a rope with your anchor line. I'll pull you on center from the stern of my boat."

He smiled slowly, surprise and pleasure lighting his face.

"Actually we don't have to go as far as Key West. If we could get it back to Tarpon Island—"

She gave him a swift look.

"It's only a few miles north around that point."

"I know, the Cameron place."

"When you get there, you can call your folks so they don't worry."

Her delicate brow darkened briefly as a cloud shadow

passing across a reef. "There's just my father. And he won't be worrying about much today."

It took a while to turn his boat and rig the line with the skiff in the lead. He steered the Mako while she maneuvered slowly to keep both boats in the deep water that circled the key until they picked up the channel. By the time they were fairly under way, it was already close to five thirty, but it was late April and Daylight Savings had started. They would have light until after seven.

The great white summer clouds piled up on the horizon. After a bit, with the skiff's forty-horsepower engine clearly managing for both boats, they both began to enjoy the trip. When the water suddenly cleared, Elissa pointed that they could see the bottom and he gave a pleased shout at the leopard ray scooting over a white sandy patch. When a ballyhoo broke the surface and skimmed through the blue air, he called out. Later they spotted a sea turtle.

"What kind is it?" he shouted.

"A hawkbill!"

"It's a great day!"

"What?" she shouted above the sound of her motor.

"Great day!"

She smiled for the first time and the smile lit the delicate bones of her face. When she turned again to her hand-bar steering, he grinned in wonder at his slender child-rescuer. With surprise he realized he was enjoying himself.

When they arrived at the Tarpon Island dock, she wanted to leave but he said, "At least come see the camp." She cast an apprehensive look toward the twenty acres of coconut palm–planted paradise with its white sand beach glittering against the blue Gulf water. Two sailboats, a catamaran, and a fifty-four foot Chris-Craft Commander were moored along the dock. The main captain's house, giddy with ship carpenter's gingerbread, shone white as a wedding cake. The guesthouses formed a small village in the palm groves. Only the Camerons would have called it a fishing camp.

So she came ashore and met the famous Camerons: Old Tom Cameron, the President-maker, still robust at seventy, who had been a wildcat oil promoter till he hit it lucky in the 1930s and invested in Manhattan real estate; his wife, Mary, with the harsh dignity of a Roman matron, whose family went back to Dutch patroons; Jim Cameron, Steve's older brother, that year founding the Museum of African Art (Old Tom funded it in return for Jim's promise to run for Senator—the secret suite, though, was Old Tom's addition, a last flowering of his scandalous virility); Jane Cameron, Jim's wife, a former film star. There were others lying around the Majorca-tiled swimming pool, planted with gardenia bushes, that wandered off from the white cane-and-wicker living room and in which various Cameron children were playing water volleyball. All were blond and handsome, with radiant Cameron smiles. Even the in-laws looked like Camerons, it seemed to Elissa. She had never before encountered the really rich, sleekly assured from the attentions of hair stylists, couturiers, orthodontists. And they were immediately friendly. She was caught by their charisma.

But neither had the Camerons met another Elissa. At twelve she was still child-slender, and the sea-shining hair curled down her tanned spine to the faded seat of her bikini. Her thunderhead eyes regarded them from some area of inner stillness as Steve related his rescue. He finished, "What's more, I don't even know her name!"

"Elissa," she said. "Elissa Blake."

"Isn't Sam Blake living in Key West now? Is there any connection?"

Elissa said, "He's my father."

Jim's wife gave a cry of recognition. The shine hadn't worn off Sam Blake's fame yet and he had not yet publicly withdrawn to cultivate his garden. Nor, for that matter, had the Camerons made their political move to the left. That curious exchange of positions came later when Old Tom broke with Nixon. At their first meeting they viewed each other across a great gulf, but they were instantly drawn to each other.

When the water volleyball game broke up, Elissa went diving with Steve and the young cousins on the coral heads beyond the little harbor. Since Sam had moved to Key West, she had been brought up in tropic waters; she sported in them like a porpoise. When Steve called her an undine, she rose with water pearling her tanned arms. "What's that?"

"A water elemental," one of the cousins explained kindly from the heights of a Groton education. And as her grave eyes continued puzzled: "It's something like a mermaid."

She spouted a crystal jet of water from her snorkel and, mute with social confusion, dived.

When she got back to the houseboat in the Key West turning basin at sunset, she found Sam at the top deck railing, holding a glass of iced coffee. A knowledgeable glance told her he was coming off his latest binge. The bony face with the long crooked nose was pale and sweating; the thin fingers gripping his coffee were shaking. But he seemed sober. And Black Bart was missing. Black Bart was a sobriety indicator. He was an ebony mongrel who had returned with Sam from one of Sam's drunks and had settled down with them as if Sam needed watching. He was a great lover, so that when Sam was sober, they rarely saw him. But when Sam was drinking he trailed him cautiously, his soft brown, strangely human eyes freighted with worry.

As she tied the skiff to the stern of the houseboat, Sam straightened his lean heron's body and she heard the familiar voice with its traces of Virginia. "Pretty late, honey, to be out running around the islands."

"I wasn't running around. I was towing a wiped-out Mako."

He whistled.

"One of the Camerons lost both lower units on a coral head. I towed him from Mud Key to Tarpon Island."

"Mighty impressive. Any trouble with the skiff?"

"No."

"Good," he said. "I'd hate to break down towing an oil criminal."

She threw her gear bag over her shoulder and jumped aboard the houseboat. Climbing the steps to the top deck, she dropped the dive bag in her bunkroom, then paused at the door to her shower.

"Why are they criminals?"

"Oil," he said. "Cameron Oil. International cartels, antitrust, price fixing, part of the military-industrial complex."

She reacted coolly, having been teethed on his anti-Vietnam stand so that she took the crimes of industry for granted. "I thought they were in politics."

"Sure. They have to legislate protection for the swag. Old Tom's even buying one of the sons a seat in the Senate."

"That must be Jim," she said. "Mine was Steve—the one I towed home. He's not much of an oil criminal. He's working for the New York District Attorney."

"Probably grooming him for President." He gave a moody sigh. "Bunch of carpetbaggers."

Recognizing that he'd slipped into his role as the Old Virginian, she wandered into the shower beside her bunkroom. As she slipped out of her bikini and washed the salt water from her hair, she compared life at Tarpon Island with the run-down houseboat of once-landed Virginia farmers. She considered her great-grandfather who had been a judge till he'd died of drink (in his daguerreotype he looked like Edgar Allan Poe), and her grandfather, an itinerant newspaperman addicted to morphine. When she came out, wrapped in a bath towel, she said, "I don't see how you call yourself a radical when you think we're so grand because we're Old Virginians."

He smiled wryly. "A fatal dichotomy, I admit. Still"—more jauntily—"you must admit that we retain, if not the virtues, the aristocratic vices."

"I don't see what's so aristocratic about being stoned. The Camerons might be oil criminals but their chrome is polished and their house is painted."

He gave her a chastened look and when she ducked back into her room and came out wearing another faded, but dry, bikini, he followed her down to the galley and watched her open a can of beans for their supper.

"If you'd give up doping—" she began as she cut up lettuce for salad.

"Absolutely no dope! Not this time! No grass, no coke, absolutely nothing!"

"Well, drink then," she said. "What's the difference? If you'd stop, you could finish the book and we could afford to paint the houseboat. We'll sink here if we don't scrape the bottom. If we got it all fixed, maybe my mother—"

"Now honey, you know it's foolish to get your hopes up."

"But it's been years. She might be—"

"That's downright senseless! You know the facts!"

"I was about to *say* that she might be anywhere," she announced with dignity. "It's ridiculous, a person not knowing where her mother is." Her voice was calm but her lips trembled.

He sighed and ran his long fingers across his sweating forehead. "Okay, honey, I'll write your Aunt Claudia."

"When?"

"I don't know." She looked at him. "All right. Tomorrow."

She lifted herself on her bare toes and kissed him. Then

she picked up two plates, forks, and stuck a bottle of catsup under one arm. "Where's Black Bart?"

"I bored him. He jumped overboard and swam ashore. I guess he's scaring up a spot of romance."

"It's hot down here. Let's eat topside tonight. Want to bring the salad?" And raising the saucepan of beans from the stove, she led the way up the galley stairs.

Despite Sam's fulminations on oil criminals, when the Cameron's Chris-Craft Commander turned up off their stern, Elissa went drift fishing with Steve and the young cousins, then back to Tarpon Island for their last fish fry of the winter season. Next day the whole family migrated north with spring.

But they didn't forget her. Mrs. Cameron shipped a great box of moistened lilacs and apple blossoms from the family home at Chadwyck-on-Hudson. Old Tom Cameron sent a gold charm from Tiffany's.

It was Steve's present, though, that changed her direction. With a card of thanks for her rescue of the Mako, he sent a 35mm Leica. It was a working professional's camera, too good for a junior high school student. But the Camerons were given to the lavish gesture.

She studied the instructions for hours before she dared her first photograph—Black Bart silhouetted by a bruised sunset. When the film was developed, it disappointed her and she went to a photographer friend of Sam's, who showed her how to use her light meter. He also gave her some filters and an old telephoto lens.

From then on she photographed everything—pelicans riding the buoys in the turning basin, a languid mutt lying in the middle of the street, white-crested pigeons filling a blue sky, ghost crabs poised on the beach at sunrise. The Leica became an icon through which she reached the radiant world of the Camerons, and she sent her best shots like propitiatory offerings to draw them back to the Florida Keys.

They did come back. All except Jim Cameron, who vanished that summer while he was collecting cult figures in Uganda. There was a headlined search and vague, terrible rumors of torture and ritual cannibalism, but no one ever learned for certain what had happened. The new African Art Museum became his memorial. Which was fitting. Despite Old Tom's ambitions for him, Jim had never really cared for politics.

After Jim's disappearance, Old Tom settled his hopes on Steve. And as the political pace quickened, he came to Tarpon Island less often. In the next seven years life swept him far from Elissa. He married a Philadelphia debutante named Cathy, had two children, ran for Governor. For two years he didn't return at all.

Then one day Elissa saw the Cameron station wagon parked outside a boutique on Duval Street and her hopes flared. The previous week she'd seen Steve's mother, who had told her Steve might be down between legislative sessions. Getting up her courage, she marched grandly into the boutique and pretended to be inspecting gold-threaded blouses marked with unbelievable price tags. But Steve hadn't been the driver of the station wagon. It was a beautiful chestnut-haired woman wearing expensive white slacks and a pale pink man's shirt, wafting a scented cloud of carnations. She was wearing a large solitaire on her wedding finger and Elissa knew at once it was Cathy Cameron. She was too awed by the vision to introduce herself.

It was Elissa's only sight of her.

And as it turned out, Steve hadn't forgotten. Though he didn't come to the keys, postcards began to turn up from the New York State capital at Albany, from skiing jaunts to Aspen, a publicized junket to the Middle East. Even when Cathy Cameron slashed her throat in a sanatorium and the funeral pictures spread across the front pages, he remembered. That Christmas a handsome book of Time-Life photographs arrived from Brentano's.

When she graduated from high school, Sam Blake seemed to arrive at a climacteric. His third book still wasn't finished. Sober, he was morose; and drunk, he grew increasingly erratic. One day he grabbed a handful of *Watchtowers* from a Jehovah's Witness on Duval Street and forced them on bystanders, his bony face wild, his pale eyes wicked above the long battered nose, until the police came and got him. Black Bart, his muzzle white now, trailed them on the old familiar way to the booking room of the courthouse. Next day, on Sam's release, he heaved himself from the shade of a poinciana tree with a jaded air.

A week later Sam tried to release the captive turtles from the tourist turtle kraals. Soon he slashed the tires of a noisy motorcycle, got beaten up, and was treated and released from the emergency ward. He spent the rest of the night maundering about artistic integrity to an exasperated Elissa, and next day, to her surprise, joined Alcoholics Anonymous.

Two months later, sober and subdued, he brought home a pleasant lady he had met at the AA meetings. Her name was Delia. She was about Sam's age, a tall brunette with a young girl's manner, who had lived in the shade of a professor father in Indiana. Instead of marrying she had taken her master's degree in music and become a closet drinker. On her father's death she had surprised all his colleagues by selling the house and following God knew what romantic dream to Key West, where she got a job teaching music in the local high school. When her drinking worsened, she joined AA and four years later when Sam turned up, she was already an old-timer. Her feeling for Sam soon neared idolatry. But as she settled onto the houseboat, tidying, cooking, and typing, she was so eager for Elissa's good opinion that she made Elissa uneasy. Only Black Bart seemed relieved to surrender the burden of Sam's future. Under Delia's cosseting he lost his anxious look and lay in the galley dreaming. He twitched as he seemed to relive old scents, exciting escapes with Sam down back alleys, and perhaps high-spirited bitches. One night, still sleeping, he sighed and died.

At that point, just as Elissa grew uncomfortable on the houseboat, a handsome pharmacist's mate stationed at the local Navy base fell in love with her and wanted them to marry. It was one solution. But her own lack of passion disturbed her. She was eighteen and had never fallen in love the way she saw that other girls did. Erotic sensations moved her only when she slept and were amorphous and indecisively directed. She was unsure which part in her dreams she was really playing.

She solved the problem with Sam Blake's own abruptness. She ran an ad in the Key West *Citizen* describing her old bottle collection and sold it for a thousand dollars. Next day she packed Sam's old suitcase, hung her Leica around her neck, and left for New York to become a photographer.

It was her first air trip. During her childhood wanderings she and her father had always traveled in a brightly painted old school bus. As the little Air Sunshine DC-3 lifted, she looked down at the keys dotting the flat turquoise and green waters of the ocean and the Gulf of Mexico. When a stewardess about her own age offered her orange juice, she was too excited to want a beverage. She admired the worldly passengers who were coolly reading newspapers. When the plane turned inland, she was still pressing her forehead to the window. It looked swampy now and she wondered if she was seeing the Everglades. Soon she saw houses looking more like Monopoly pieces than real houses, blue swimming pools, and beetlelike cars traveling along a freeway. Then they slanted toward the earth of Miami airport. She held her breath till she felt a bump, machinery screamed, and after endless moments, she felt their brakes begin to catch.

During her holdover in Miami she wandered the airport with a sense of being propelled into her future. She inspected the exotic destinations posted above the airline counters, scouted a vast bookstore, and purchased a box of chocolate-covered turtles. An hour before her next departure she was already sitting at the gate.

On the Delta flight she had a glass of free champagne and a steak lunch and a meringue tart on a plastic tray. Then, as they were flying too high to see more than clouds, she read a copy of *The New Yorker* in a leather airline cover until the captain announced they were approaching the Potomac. Soon after that they descended into the opaque air of New York.

Following signs and listening for the loudspeaker announcements, she found the luggage section, secured Sam's bag, slung Sam's old parka about her shoulders to prepare for the January weather, and made her way to the buses heading for the city.

The cloverleafs around JFK amazed her, and so did the traffic, but she was disappointed by the ugly duplex houses that lined the freeways. Then disillusion evaporated: She realized the dingy patches in front of the houses were actual snow.

It was rush hour when they pulled into the East Side terminal. She got her bag from the bus driver and pressed through the crowd looking for taxis. She planned to take a cab to a Greenwich Village hotel that Sam remembered, where she would stay till she could find an apartment and sign up for courses at The New School. But a boy in jeans, carrying a guitar, beat her to the first one, and a Japanese couple got the second.

She noticed a dark boy coming toward her, glaring and muttering obscenities, and she wondered why he should be so angry at a stranger. She had a prickling sense of nearing disaster but it was still unfocused when he grabbed her shoulder bag. Instantly he was running away.

She shouted, "Hey! Don't!" But she was hampered by Sam's suitcase and couldn't catch him before he'd darted through the crowd and vanished.

She stood stunned. A few people stopped to stare at her. "My purse. He took my purse," she told them.

An elderly man shook his head in sympathy, but no one spoke and after a moment they all moved on.

She stood helpless in the human current while her shock thinned and the realization struck her: She had lost her bottle collection money, the thousand dollars that was to have enrolled her in her photography class and tided her over till she found a job.

She located a policeman. He took down her report but he was bored, even disapproving. She should have known better than to carry cash, he said. She shouldn't have carried it all in one place. He didn't actually say so, but he clearly felt it was her own fault.

Then he asked for her local address. With a threatened sense, she gave him Aunt Claudia's.

"You can catch a bus on Fifth Avenue," he said, and then a disturbance on the street caught his attention and he had to hurry off.

She found some change in her jeans pockets and considered calling Aunt Claudia. They had never met but she had always been an exotic figure in Elissa's daydreams —the beautiful rock singer who'd given up singing to help with illness in her family. When Elissa was small, Claudia had sent presents on birthdays and at Christmas. But she'd disapproved of Sam's part in the trouble with Elissa's mother, who was her younger sister, and for years she hadn't answered Sam's letters. Still, Claudia might not include her only niece in the disapproval. Deciding to call, she looked up the number in the Manhattan directory. But to her surprise, she found Claudia's phone had been disconnected.

She sat on a bench and tried to plan her next move. She hated the idea of calling Sam for a return ticket. It seemed so stupid to lose her money before she'd had a chance at the city. Perhaps, she thought, something would turn up. She began to grasp at the wild hope that the angry boy would be struck by a change of heart and bring back the bag with the money.

Night fell as she postponed a decision. The rush hour crowds dwindled, later swelled for the night flights, slackened, dwindled again. Around midnight, moved by hunger, she lugged Sam's suitcase down the street to a Nedick's and spent the change she had in her jeans pocket on a frankfurter and a Coca-Cola.

Toward morning she was herself picked up by the bus terminal police.

It was at the station house, when they were pressing her to call Sam, that desperation forced out the name of Steve Cameron. He lived upstate, of course, which wasn't the same as New York City, but after all, he was Governor and her knowing him might divert them from calling Sam while she thought of how to reach Aunt Claudia. With an amused air the sergeant called the Governor's office in Albany. He wasn't there but a secretary promised to get back to them. It ended with their seating Elissa in the squad room.

Her childhood with an anti-Establishment radical who was constantly being booked for drunkenness and destruction of private property like turtle kraals and noisy motorcycles had left her with a general sense of outlawry. When a detective brought her a Danish and coffee, her spirits lifted at his kindness, but soon she was again glancing at the Men Wanted posters and feeling a natural alliance with forgers, robbers, and the young bombers of government installations. Then suddenly Governor Cameron came breezing in.

"Elissa!" He grinned and as she got up, he put his arms about her, kissed the top of her head, and hugged her.

He was older but even more handsome, the blue gaze more brilliant, the smile more dazzling. He had arrived trailing staff members—his secretary had phoned his limousine as he headed toward New York from Albany— and he radiated the golden aura of the very rich.

He solved her problems quickly. In half an hour she had a job as a staff photographer with his New York headquarters in his campaign for the presidential primaries. She had an apartment in one of the Cameron real estate holdings in Greenwich Village. And she had three hundred dollars that he borrowed from his staff as an advance on her salary to enroll in The New School.

"Anything else?" he asked, and overwhelmed by executive power, she mutely shook her head.

"See she gets a cab to that address in the Village," he ordered the sergeant. Then he gave her another hug and said, "See you Monday."

As he swept out, the squad room seemed to dim.

After a long while she stirred in the wicker chair in her shabby little apartment, remembering they would be expecting her at campaign headquarters. She rose and made herself a cup of instant coffee. But as she stood at the kitchen drainboard, a frown drew her brows together and she turned and consulted a city map.

Steadied by decision, she showered, dressed again, hunted till she found a subway token, and set out on her way to work.

Chapter 4

Steve Cameron's New York headquarters took up the ground floor of an office building near Columbus Circle. Bunting, slogans, and posters covered the walls and plate glass windows. Desks covered the red carpeting, phones rang incessantly, and staff and volunteers swept in and out.

While Elissa was checking her desk to be sure her cameras were both still where she had left them when Steve had led her off to celebrate her birthday the previous evening—besides her old Leica, she now had a new Nikon—she found a note that her noon session to photograph Jim Cameron's widow at an East Side Golden Age Club had been canceled. So she went to the printing service around the corner and picked up the prints of the negatives she had left off the previous day.

When she got back, she found Jay Dolan, Steve's campaign manager, standing accusingly by her desk.

"Just breezing in?" he asked.

"I was picking up the Hunter College rally prints," she said, trying to resist his talent for flustering her.

He set down her purse with the air of a prosecuting attorney. "Steve gave me this."

"Thanks," she said, hating herself for blushing. "Did he get off on time for Boston?"

"He was a bit frayed but he made the plane."

She forced herself to steadiness beneath the dark, intense gaze directed through the smoke of the cigarette ever-present between his lips. Cigarette ash was already spilling down his expensive suit. Lean, wiry, with the quick, aggressive movements of the street fighter, he struck her again by his contrast to the easy, graceful Camerons. She'd heard he was brilliant, a masterly campaign strategist who had worked for Kennedy in 1968 and joined Old Tom Cameron's staff when Jim Cameron agreed to run for Senator before he was lost in Africa. And he had helped Old Tom persuade Steve to run for Governor. It was he who set the breakneck pace for their campaign. She felt he cared more for the presidency than Steve did, more than anyone perhaps except Old Tom Cameron, and she wondered what made Jay Dolan run. His own father had been a New York patrolman who had taken a law degree at night. The drive might have come from his father. But Steve's continued fondness for him surprised her.

Perhaps, she thought, it wasn't fondness so much as admiration. Jay worked constantly, sixteen to eighteen hours a day, dealing with all their primary headquarters— the press used the term workaholic. As far as she knew, he'd never visited the camp at Tarpon Island, never skied, never sailed or played handball. She thought she'd heard he played a cutthroat pool game, but otherwise, his profession, hobby, all his life, was work.

She'd have expected his irascibility would have made trouble with Steve. Jay snapped at the staff, was publicly impatient with his pretty wife—even worse from a politi-cian's viewpoint, he was often dangerously sardonic with the press.

Perhaps it was Jay's loyalty that made Steve overlook his temperamental vices. For loyal he was, like a fierce Doberman that gives allegiance to one master.

"Did you have a big night?" he asked, unable to control his curiosity.

"No, it was my birthday," she said. And under the pressure of his will for her to continue: "He took me to dinner." Then, refusing to let him bully her, she stopped.

"Well, he looked frayed, and I don't like it. He's going to need his strength for Massachusetts," he began, bearing down on her with disapproval.

They were interrupted by the state coordinator, who shouted for help with schedule trouble. And then the Saturday volunteers began arriving. In the confusion she picked up her shoulder bag and slipped out a side door.

Outside, she stopped, slid her hand in her bag, and found the little bronze water spirit Steve had given her. It shone in the daylight, small breasts bare, its fishtail flirting in a graceful movement. It felt smooth and comforting to her palm as, holding it like a touchstone, she walked quickly up the block to the subway.

She boarded an express as its doors were closing. While the car rocketed uptown, she gazed out at the passing local platforms and her face, reflected in the dirty window, was set in the composure of decision.

At 125th Street she got out, climbed the subway steps, and caught a bus marked Ward's Island.

The bus was crowded and she stood steadying herself on the overhead bar while she examined the other passengers: sad-faced black and Puerto Rican women looking as if they'd made this trip too often, boys in jeans and leather jackets, an old white woman in a worn coat with a shabby velvet collar. Some held shopping bags; most carried brown parcels. As they left Harlem for the Triborough Bridge, the sun appeared and caught the ruffled chop of the East River. In the middle of the water she could see an island with trees, grass, brick buildings, and she guessed it was Manhattan State Hospital.

Soon the bus wound down a ramp and pulled into a parking lot piled with dirty snow. The bus passengers pressed her down the bus steps and forward toward a dingy building marked Dunlap Pavilion. The wide front steps were thronged with patients wandering listlessly about in the chill February sunshine. Some were in sweaters and coats; some were in flannel bathrobes. Their faces were bored, and as the busload of visitors went off, leaving Elissa alone with them, they began to move in and circle her hopefully. An old man made a smoking gesture.

"I'm sorry," she said. "I don't smoke."

But they continued to gather like fish coming to chum. A soft hand touched her long hair. The old man made the smoking sign more insistently. When she saw a white-coated orderly, she broke from the circle and ran to him.

"I've come to see a patient," she said.

He was black, young, and seemed alive in a different way from the wandering patients or their worn visitors. "Call Information. There's a phone in that building."

She hurried by the men in bathrobes before they could surround her again and entered the Dunlap Pavilion. At the end of a corridor she found a phone and asked for Veronica Blake.

After a long pause Information said, "She's not listed."

"She might be using Veronica Verrick."

"Wait a minute." Information seemed rough and harried, though perhaps it was just the New York manner. But when she came back, she had found her.

Elissa stopped an aide for directions, then went down a long hall till she came to a bank of elevators. She rode up and when she told a nurse she wanted to see Veronica Verrick, she was sent to a little waiting room where a television set chattered beneath a steel-meshed view of sunlit Manhattan. From the middle of the river the buildings had the flat look of a child's drawing.

There already were three people in the waiting room— a leather-jacketed youngster speaking rapid Spanish to a withered old lady in a bathrobe, and on a plastic chair opposite, another old woman from the bus, still clutching the handle of her shopping bag. Elissa smiled at her but the old woman averted her gaze and Elissa went back to the view out the window. Once an attendant came in, consulted a clipboard, then wandered out again. The television set ran through commercials on dish powder, a floor wax, and dog food, and began a 1950s movie. Finally a black nurse ushered in another old woman.

"Elissa Blake?" the nurse asked, and as Elissa rose unsurely, the nurse led the other woman to her.

For a long moment they stood facing each other, the tall young girl with the cascade of bright hair and the old woman in the faded bathrobe. Then the woman smiled shyly. Elissa put out her hand and Veronica grasped it. Her hand felt like the paw of a timid animal. Elissa embraced her and Veronica nuzzled against her. When they separated, her smile was broader, so that Elissa saw the missing front teeth. Then, moved by some dimly remembered vanity, Veronica ducked her head in an evasive movement and her lips hid the gap.

"She got teeth, she just don't like to wear them. They good about giving out teeth here," the nurse said, as if Elissa had accused her.

But Veronica's gaze had already slid past Elissa to the view beyond the window.

"Let's sit her down," the nurse said. "Then you have yourself a little visit." She led Veronica to a plastic chair and Veronica sat down and scratched at her ankle. The skin on her legs was paper-white.

Elissa tried for words to fill the terrible silence, but the shock of seeing the actual Veronica was so great that she could find no words. Desperation grew in her.

Seeing Elissa's drawn face, the nurse lingered. "They said at the desk she's your mother." And as Elissa mutely nodded, "I don't think I see you here before. This your first time?"

Elissa said guiltily, "I've been in Florida. I was only six when she . . ." She trailed off. "I haven't seen her in twelve years."

"You don't want to feel bad about that, child. Some folks don't come at all. You here now. That's a nice thing," the nurse said. And as Veronica continued to look toward the window, "Florida, is that a fact? I got a daughter in Perrine—that's near Miami."

Elissa's gaze slid back to Veronica. She saw she wasn't really old, though the shining hair had dulled and was cut short now; her cheeks were covered with tiny wrinkles like the skin on hot milk. The faded blue gaze wandered back from the window and Veronica smiled again, vaguely.

The nurse said, "This here your daughter, Veronica. What's your name again?"

"Elissa."

"This here's your own child, Veronica." The brown eyes that met Elissa's were filled with meaning. "She been here a long time, know what I mean? Them days, they got like agitated—" She stopped as if Elissa should realize something, but Elissa only frowned with incomprehension.

"Like today they mostly give them medication. Them days, they, you know, operated—"

"I don't understand."

"I try to tell you, they done them lobotomies."

"Is that where they . . . cut out—?" Elissa stopped.

"Only a partial. She only had a partial. They didn't do it here. Someplace before she got here."

Elissa looked down at her slender fingers, then looked up, expressionless. "They destroyed her brain."

The nurse was silent.

"She was so lovely. Even her hair—I used to play with it. It fell to her waist."

"Course it a long time, twelve years," the nurse said gently. "You gonna find out yourself what the years do."

"But to operate—cut her brain—"

"Were she agitated?"

Elissa nodded slowly. "At the end, before she ran away— That's why our names are different. She must have taken her maiden name again." But distress again overwhelmed her.

"See, if she were making herself real unhappy—you know, seeing things that wasn't there, shouting at them, maybe getting violent—"

"She saw things that used to frighten her."

"Well, the doctors back then, they might have done it."

"I can still hear her, the way she used to scream."

Clouds were streaming across the sun when she left the hospital, and as she rode the bus back across the bridge, the river darkened so that its surface was almost black. Elissa shivered and huddled in her seat, trying to replace the picture of the faded woman in the waiting room with the sunlit blond mother she remembered from her childhood.

But she herself had been so young, she could only recall it like pieces of a jigsaw puzzle: a laughing woman on a psychedelic-painted bus nibbling peyote buttons, laying her shining head on a man's shoulder. (Had it been Sam? Had he once had a moustache?) A glimpse of cliff dropping sheer to the water in the Big Sur country; Monterey pines beyond their redwood house; a big room with Madras spreads for room dividers; crowds of bearded youths and girls in Indian headbands; and Veronica bending over her, lovely, smiling, ankle bells tinkling, smelling of sandalwood.

How old was I? Elissa wondered. Four? Five? Veronica

must have been twenty-two then, not much more than she herself was now. The thought was stunning. She sat not seeing beyond the dirty bus window as the scenes changed, splintering like a slow-motion smashing of a mirror.

She was leading Veronica along a cliff. (Where was Sam? In New York, with his first book?) A vague, strange Veronica. Then Veronica curled up in a corner on the floor, Veronica crying, beating against a window-pane, desperately sobbing. (What was that? Mescaline? LSD?) Had Veronica believed herself a bird trapped in the redwood house? They had been heavy into hallu-cinogens in Big Sur. Too heavy for a young, suddenly famous novelist trying to start on a new book. Too many drugs, too many people, too much trouble with Veronica.

Abruptly, in the Sam Blake manner, they picked up and headed east. For a while they swung aimlessly about the country. Then they bought a houseboat off Key West.

It had been like waking from fever dreams into sunshine. The keys were blue sky, bright warm water, blossoming trees. A wondrous stillness descended on them.

Sitting on the bus, that stillness still moved her, the sense of inner center reached, a quiet radiance. They had anchored the houseboat off a place called Wisteria Island. At night the lights of Key West trailed bright ribbons across the calm water. Music drifted from shore. They heard schools of mullet jumping. Heat lightning lit up deserted islands on the horizon. Elissa remembered how she felt then, as if she'd moved and existed in light.

But the respite didn't last. Veronica's visions began again. She stood at the houseboat railing, staring with horror out at the water, refusing to tell them what she was seeing.

For a while Sam tried to reason her out of the unnamed terror. He searched the houseboat for hidden drugs but found nothing, no mescaline, no LSD, no peyote. And she had never been much of a drinker; it wasn't delirium tremens. He had to give up the hope of a chemical solution.

She wasn't eating and she slept badly. None of them were sleeping for that matter.

One night when she was six, Elissa wakened to the sound of whimpering. Rolling out of her bunk, she padded to the houseboat's top deck and found Veronica standing by the railing. Her long pale hair shone, her white caftan stirred in clear moonlight as she pressed to the rail, staring out over the water. It was she who was whimpering. Elissa came to her and asked, "What's the matter, mommy?"

Veronica whispered, "See the evil insects—crawling across the water."

Elissa followed her gaze but all she saw was the smooth surface of the turning basin. The tide was swinging them at anchor so that the dark trees of Wisteria Island lay on their left; mooring lights glowed from the little flotilla of boats that lay between them and the island of Key West. Guitar music came softly to them from a shabby Bahamian sloop lying to their starboard. She heard the sad, deep note of the Sylvia buoy that had been named for a local nightclub pianist.

Veronica raised pale fingers to her ears and whispered, "They're crawling in my ears." Her beautiful face was anguished. "They're trying to get into my brain."

Elissa pressed her small naked body to Veronica, clinging to her and trying to calm her. But Veronica pushed her off with a quick movement and began hawking and spitting into the turning basin as if she were ridding herself of the invisible insects. When she paused, exhausted, and gave a strange, wild cry of frustration, Elissa ran to her parents' bunkroom and woke Sam.

He was a younger Sam then, tall, wiry, but already stress was carving his face into the mask of a man much older. His nose had already been broken on an epic drunk, too. He came on deck barefooted, fastening a patched pair of jeans, took hold of his wife's shoulders, holding her to him as he tried to reason with her. But she pushed him away as she'd pushed away Elissa, tore at her long hair, brushed at her ears with crazy movements, finally started a terrible screaming. A light came on in the Bahamian sloop to their starboard.

"What's up, man?" Sam's friend Coconut Charley called.

"I need help," Sam shouted.

He grabbed Veronica again, and before she could resist, got her down the houseboat stairs and grappled her into the skiff tied up to their stern. Shocked, Elissa watched from the top of the houseboat as Veronica screamed and began thrashing to free herself. The skiff nearly upset and Sam struck her. Then he set her down, sobbing, and started up the little motor.

"Charley!" he shouted.

"Right here, man! Got you covered!"

Sam steered the skiff to Charley's sloop, and as he pulled alongside, Coconut Charley jumped into the skiff wearing only a seashell necklace and the satin shorts his lady had made for him.

"You stay put now! I'll be right back. Be a good girl!" Sam yelled to Elissa as she watched them head for shore.

She saw them beach. Sam was staying in the skiff with her mother while Charley sprinted into the darkness.

Soon a patrol car bumped across the marl to the beached skiff. Veronica's screams came clearly across the water as Sam, Charley, and two policemen wrestled her into the patrol car and drove off.

For what seemed forever, Elissa waited alone on the houseboat. She searched the surface of the water for the evil insects and couldn't understand why she couldn't see them. She tried to comprehend, too, why her father hadn't fought the police but even helped when they carried off her mother. She already knew Sam as a cop fighter. At last, in devastation, she went down and curled up in her parents' bunk to comfort herself with the familiar smell of their bodies.

She was still there when she heard the skiff returning. Jumping up, she ran to the top deck railing. But the skiff contained only Sam and Coconut Charley.

As Sam dropped Charley off at his sloop, she saw Charley clap a sympathetic hand on Sam's shoulder and say to him, "It's a bummer."

Then Sam moved off toward their houseboat. He was tying up when she got downstairs again.

"Where's my mommy?" she asked.

"Mommy's at the hospital. She's sick," he said.

"When will she be back?"

"Soon, honey. Soon."

But she wasn't. A week later she was admitted to the state hospital at Chattahoochee.

Veronica never forgave Sam for the betrayal. A month later Coconut Charley and his tanned, bikini-clad lady stayed with Elissa while Sam visited Veronica. Elissa was sure he'd bring her back. But when Sam finally appeared on shore at sunset two days later, Veronica wasn't with him.

Charley took Elissa to shore in the skiff and the tatterdemalion crowd that ritually appeared to watch the sun slide into the Gulf of Mexico held the boat while Sam tottered toward them. They saw he had been drinking.

"What happened, man?" asked Charley.

"She wouldn't see me," Sam answered. He shook his head to clear his vision, then clambered blearily into the skiff. "The doctors said I'd have to wait. They didn't want to press her."

"No good to press her. The only thing that heals is love, man."

"But what if I can't see her?"

"Wait and give it another try," Charley said.

But when Sam phoned the hospital before his next trip, he was told Veronica still didn't want to see him.

At last the medication worked and Veronica was released to go back to New York and help her sister, who was nursing their dying mother. Soon the trouble flared again and Veronica began the round of New York state hospitals—Hudson River Valley, Rockland, Pilgrim State. Sam and Elissa traced her progress through Claudia's letters until word from Claudia herself grew fitful.

When she was twelve, just before she met Steve Cameron, Elissa herself wrote to Veronica's last known address. But she got no answer. At the end of a month's waiting, Sam found her crying in her bunk. It was during one of his periods of sobriety and with a few questions he homed in on the reason. Helplessly he stroked her hair and finally held her.

"You've got to let go of that one, sweetheart."

Elissa's voice was muffled against his chest. "But she's my mother! What if she's in some terrible place hoping I'll come and find her?"

"When she was here, hon, we couldn't help her."

For a long moment she absorbed this. Finally she swiped at her tears and sat up. "What went wrong with her? What happened?"

He considered. "Maybe acid."

"Was she taking it?"

"I didn't find anything when I looked. But you can trip out long after you've quit taking it." A look of pain crossed his ruined features. "In the beginning we didn't know about that."

"But you took it! You're all right!" In the silence neither mentioned his drinking, the dabbling in drugs, or his recent agonizing bouts with writer's block.

"Maybe it was some chemical or psychological imbalance that the LSD triggered."

"Then if I took it—she's my mother—do you think I've maybe inherited—"

"Quit that morbid nonsense!" Sam flashed in anger. "You're a perfectly healthy, normal girl," he said more quietly.

"But wasn't she healthy? Was there anything wrong with her?"

He sighed, got up from the bunk, and stared at the blue water blazing outside her window.

"What about Grandma Verrick? Wasn't there something funny?"

"There was absolutely nothing wrong with the Verricks," Sam said in the loud, dogged voice he used when he was lying. And he flatly refused to be drawn further, which left her with the sense that there had indeed been something queer about the Verricks.

Then Claudia Verrick ceased writing entirely and they gradually accepted the fact that they'd lost track of Veronica. It was not till last week that Elissa had finally found her.

On her afternoon off the previous Saturday, she had looked for Claudia at the Christopher Street address given in the phone book. It was a shabby brick tenement not far from her own apartment on Waverly Place. Television antennas bristled among its chimney pots; a fire escape ran down its front.

An elderly woman in a brown crocheted cap was taking the winter sun before an open window.

Elissa studied the row of battered mailboxes in the foyer till she found VERRICK—1c scrawled on a torn scrap of paper stuck into the nameplate. But when she pressed the buzzer, the bell system seemed to be out of order. The lock on the front door was also broken, however, and she let herself in and went down the dark hallway past crayoned walls to 1C.

When she knocked, there was no answer, nor a sense

of presence from inside the apartment. She slowly returned to the front of the tenement, trying to decide if she should leave a note, and the old woman in the crocheted cap leaned out her window. "The lock's broke. The kids break it," she called out. "Who do you want?"

"Miss Verrick in One-C."

"Verrick," the old woman said. The silence between them was thick with bill collectors and collection agencies.

"She's my aunt. She wasn't expecting me," Elissa said. "I've been living in Florida."

"Florida," the old woman repeated as if weighing the word for Elissa's true intentions. "How come your aunt didn't know you was coming?"

"I tried to call but her phone is disconnected."

"Don't they teach you how to write in Florida?" And when Elissa smiled helplessly, "You got a tan. I'll give you that. That hair of yours its real color?"

Elissa nodded.

"Your aunt's sure ain't. Try the Greenwich movie theater. She sometimes works the matinee."

Elissa found it hard to connect the lovely rock singer whose photographs she had seen in her childhood with the rough champagne blonde behind the box office glass. Claudia's skin had a boiled look; a vein pulsed at her temple. Since the movie had already started, business was slow and she was working the *Daily News* crossword puzzle. Remembering that Claudia had once sent her a crossword puzzle book—at ten, it had been a disappointing present—Elissa approached and asked unsurely, "Aunt Claudia?"

The raw-boned blonde looked up from her paper.

"I'm Elissa. Veronica's daughter."

The hazy blue eyes focused. "Elissa?"

"Aren't you my aunt? My mother's sister?"

"Elissa! Hey, how about that! How come you're here?"

"I'm studying photography. I've got a job, too—"

"I can't believe it. Where's your father?"

"He's still living in Key West."

"I haven't heard from him in years. What's he up to these days? Remarried?"

"Not exactly. He's got a lady but I guess he's still actually married to my mother. I wondered how I could find her."

"Veronica?" The sudden change in her was disconcerting. The blue stare, too vague at first, was now too intense. Elissa had seen the manner before but at first she couldn't place it. Then she recalled Sam's speed-freak visitors hopped up on Dexedrine or meth. As Claudia hunched closer to the box office window, Elissa stepped back. Sam always said he was afraid of speed freaks.

"Your mother's a sick woman."

"Yes, well, I thought I could go and see her."

"She was *damaged* before she came back here. I don't know what it was your father did—"

"He didn't do anything!"

"He threw her into an insane asylum."

"She was seeing . . . things. She might have hurt herself."

Claudia didn't seem to hear. "Right when our mother was dying of brain cancer. I had to give up my singing to nurse them."

That part was true. Claudia had been a rising young rock singer in the early 1960s. Elissa had once had a poster in her bunkroom which read: CLAUDIA VER-RICK and THE GRAVESTONES at the TULSA CIVIC CENTER. She had toured the country, cut some records, had been booked to appear at a Monterey festival when her mother fell ill.

"You can't imagine what it was like, the two of them screaming—" The force of the past seemed to break loose and strike her. When a customer asked for a ticket, she had trouble making change, and when she returned to Elissa, the silent pursuit of her thoughts had made her angry. "Mother was tough enough before her sickness."

Elissa understood. In the 1920s her grandmother, Elinor

Verrick, had been a wild Greenwich Village poet. She wrote that her life was a flame, and gave birth to two illegitimate children—Claudia by a sculptor, and Veronica by a once-famous writer who died on the Bowery. In her last years she took dictation from Byron on a planchette. No wonder Claudia had run off with a guitarist and Veronica had eloped at sixteen with Sam Blake.

"I had no choice. The yelling and shrieking—the neighbors pounding on the wall. Mother lost control of her functions. I had to do it."

"Do what?"

"Call for help, of course. What would *you* do? They put them both into Bellevue. Mother died and they sent Veronica to Rockland. You haven't any right to blame me." It was as if it had all happened yesterday instead of twelve years ago.

"I'm not blaming you. Honestly. Is that where she is now? In Rockland?"

"No, I wrote your father all about it. After Rockland, it was Hudson Valley. Then Pilgrim State."

"Where is she now, Aunt Claudia?"

"Nobody could have stood the two of them."

"I know you tried," Elissa said, trying to reach her through the fog of guilt.

But Claudia responded only within her own torment. She glared at Elissa and suddenly snapped, "Are you okay?"

"Sure. Why?"

"Because you look exactly like her. Two peas in a pod, you and Veronica." The raddled face glinted with malice. The abrupt switch from guilt to attack caught Elissa off guard and her unease increased. Still, it was the only thread that led to Veronica. In the back of her mind she still cherished the hope that if she could find Veronica, her own health might heal her.

She said, "I still want to see her."

"Then try Manhattan State," Claudia said, dismissing

her. It was as if in choosing her sister, Elissa had rejected her. "You'll be sorry. She was always peculiar. She took after mother. You're sure you're all right, you don't see things yourself?" The sly glint was back.

"I'm fine," Elissa answered firmly.

But that had been before the night in the museum.

As she got off the Ward's Island bus and headed downtown in the subway, she kept trying to erase the pictures: Claudia's eyes sharp with jealous spite, and her mother, the frail, dulled woman with the missing teeth. But when, with enormous effort, she managed to erase them, she was back in the secret suite standing above Steve's blood-soaked body, hearing the sound of her own queer whisper at the scene that hadn't really taken place.

It was nearly five o'clock by the time she got out at the West Fourth Street station and climbed the subway stairs into the raw February evening. The Saturday night crowds were already starting to wander through the porous snow piled up in the gutters before the newspaper kiosk. All the faces seemed pale and unhealthy from city living. Everyone was swaddled in heavy coats, woolen scarves, and clumsy, heavy galoshes. A bus stopped, spraying her with dirty slush, and she read the ad that ran along its side: FLY EASTERN TO THE FLORIDA SUN. For a moment she thought of sunshine, the blue Gulf waters, green mangrove islands, and homesickness engulfed her. She hungered to be diving for conch and sand dollars and sea fans, watching the bright reef fish duck in and out among the coral branches. And she was only three and a half hours from it. If she jumped in a taxi and headed for the airport, she could be back on the houseboat by bedtime, rocked toward sleep by the wakes of passing shrimp boats. Then she remembered that Sam had written he'd moved the houseboat from the turning basin to the yacht club so Delia wouldn't have to use the skiff to go to work every morning. There would no longer be a wake from passing shrimp boats. Still, when she woke, she could throw her gear into the skiff, start up the old motor, and take off on a long golden day of water, sky, and healing silence.

Only too much had changed. Sam had Delia now, who would be wounded if she didn't wait for a real breakfast. And she was nineteen; it was time to keep a job and support herself. But more important than all that was Steve Cameron.

Sometimes she thought of love as like being shot with a spear gun. No matter how she twisted, the spear was embedded and the cord held. She couldn't free herself to return to the peace of her childhood. And yet she knew that Steve hadn't really done it; she had fallen in love with him all by herself.

Actually she didn't even know when it had happened, whether it had been the day in the precinct house when he had effortlessly solved her problems, or whether it was sometime during the years since he had stopped coming to Tarpon Island. It was as if during the long daydream of her adolescence, she had drifted into a whirlpool that moved her in quickening circles around the Camerons, till at the end, the Camerons had turned out to mean only Steve.

The night of her birthday he had sensed her feeling. At dinner overlooking the park and the lights of the city, and later when he had given her the little water spirit, his presence had buoyed her, made her strangely joyful, so that she glowed in a new way and he saw her differently. Swept on by the strength of her feeling, he showed her the secret spring, and like children they had entered the museum suite, made drinks and toasted his campaign for President, almost without words embraced and moved into the bedroom. She hadn't minded the brief pain, just as she was too overwhelmed to climax by the wonder of his nearness. That could come later, in some future when she would grow more used to him. If there was a future.

The thought chilled her as she moved through the slush. If he hadn't regretted the night when he woke next morning. He hadn't sounded it, but how could she really tell? And what if she were pregnant? He had probably assumed she was on the pill until he realized it was her first time. But by then it was too late to stop.

The worst fear was that she was following Veronica into hallucination. She paused on the pavement, remembering Steve's body on the bed. It came back to her as clearly as a real memory. Wasn't hallucinating a sign of madness? And wasn't it likely with her family background? Aunt Claudia seemed peculiar, too. At the very least, she acted like she was on speed. And there was her grandmother, Elinor Verrick of the crazy Village years, the love children, the planchette dictation from Lord Byron. Even her cancer had chosen the brain as if fastening on existing derangement—

"That's nonsense," she told herself resolutely. Mental illness wasn't like asbestos or tobacco irritation. You didn't get brain cancer from mental illness. She entered a grocery store and bought frozen pizza and salad greens for dinner.

When she came out, a cold drizzle was falling. The street lights shone on wet pavement. Shielding her grocery bag, she hurried toward Waverly Place.

As she let herself in the front door of her building, a man was standing at the elevator. He opened the elevator door and waved her ahead of him. When she said "Four, please," he pressed the button.

It wasn't till the gate had closed that she sensed something wrong about him. Her first blurred impression was of a young, slight-built stranger in a crumpled shirt and leather jacket. But as the elevator began to creak toward her top-floor apartment, the vague sense of wrongness made her cut her gaze across him and she saw that he was sweating. Big drops of sweat beaded his forehead. Perhaps he was ill, she thought, or drugged. There were a lot of addicts in the Village. Jenny didn't use the washing machines in the basement because they crept in to sleep by the furnace. The super was supposed to keep them out but he was careless.

The man cleared his throat and asked, "You live on the top floor?"

She nodded, then stared straight ahead, watching the steel elevator doors slip past them. She felt faintly guilty about being so unfriendly. In Key West you talked to everybody. And he might be just ill or lonely. But Jenny was firm about not talking to strangers. She was still watching the passing doors when she heard the voices.

A man's voice was saying, "I've got a knife. Don't scream or I'll have to kill you."

She froze and glanced at the man in the leather jacket, but he didn't seem to have spoken.

Then a strangled gasp and a girl's voice murmured, "Don't, oh please don't."

Elissa thought that perhaps they were overhearing people talking on the floor they were passing. Still, that was impossible—the sound was beside her.

"Come on. I told you, don't give me no trouble."

Fear rose about her as she heard a confused blend of murmurs, gasps, and a sound like bodies bumping against the plywood elevator paneling.

"Not like that!" the girl's voice pleaded.

A whispered litany of obscenity was cut off by a scream. Then the scream stopped abruptly.

The most horrible thing was that there was no girl. The man and herself were riding alone in the elevator.

She glanced again toward the man to see if he had heard anything. But before she could tell, he slipped his hand into his pocket and blind panic swept over her. Without planning, not knowing what she did, she pressed the Stop button.

"This isn't your floor!" he protested.

The elevator gate was already opening. She pushed out the steel door and scrambled down over the uneven landing.

"Hey!" the man yelled.

She saw the number on Jenny's door, ran, and pounded on it. Al Martin pulled it open and stood towering in the doorway, his black fringe wild about his balding head. "Elissa!"

She threw her arms about him, dropping her groceries. "A man!"

She heard the elevator door slam behind her, then the grinding noise of the metal gate closing.

"You have trouble with somebody?" Al asked.

But what could she actually tell him? That a man had put his hand into his pocket?

"I don't know. I heard—it sounds so crazy."

He loosed her hold on him, held her from him, and looked down into her face. His gentle brown eyes grew troubled. "Come in. Tell us about it. Take your time."

He picked up her groceries. Then putting his other arm about her shoulders, he shut the door and walked her into the apartment. "Jen!"

Elissa stopped when she saw the living room. The lamps were lit and drapes were drawn against the dusky drizzle. The bookshelves were straightened, the pillows plumped on the Victorian sofa. The cobbler's bench and coffee table glowed with polish. The folding table had been opened and covered with a white tablecloth. A bowl of daffodils was set in the middle.

"You're having company!"

"Just Don," Al said. "You know, my professor. Jenny spent the day calling Cameron's headquarters to ask you to come, too. Didn't you get her messages?"

"I was—" But the memory of Manhattan State overwhelmed her and she finished lamely, "I was out."

"Well, you're here now." And he swept her into the

kitchen where Jenny was poking something in the oven.

"Hi," she said, turning, and then at the sight of Elissa's face, "What happened?"

"I heard—" Elissa started and stopped, unable to describe it.

Al said, "I think she had a scare in the elevator."

"I heard, well, voices. A man raped a girl."

Jenny said, "Call the police, Al!"

"Wait!" Elissa pleaded. "I just heard their voices. He said he had a knife but it was only in my head." She looked miserably from one to the other. "There wasn't any other girl either."

Jenny and Al exchanged glances. She knew by the exchange that Al had heard about her seeing Steve's murder. She thought of Veronica, the blue eyes dulled, the bright hair faded, shuffling into the waiting room, and she cried, "You think I'm going crazy!"

Jenny put her arms around her.

"What's crazy, Elissa?" Al asked. "It's just a word. Listen, hon, everybody fantasizes. Last night on our way home in the subway, I saw this mean-looking guy and I fantasized he tried to mug me. I slugged him and we had a big knockdown fight. Pow, I socked him right off the subway platform. It was a whole long fantasy. There's nothing wrong with that. You've just got to know it's not really happening."

"But I heard voices. And my family—" She hesitated. It was too painful to speak of the notorious Elinor Verrick, of Aunt Claudia, or her mother. "I think I'd better go. I'm not really hungry and with another person—"

Jenny hugged her. "It's just Don. And wait till you see what I've cooked. Pot roast and apple pie. Come on, Elissa—you'll make Don so happy. He loves pretty girls."

Elissa smiled a bit unsurely as Al took her parka and

Jenny led her into the kitchen and laid out a bowl, a knife, greens, tomatoes, and cucumbers.

"Here. Create," she said. "Make the salad."

Jenny poured her a glass of rosé while Al went to the living room and put a Mozart quintet on the stereo. Elissa stored her own pizza and lettuces in the refrigerator, and with the silvery music shimmering about her, she began to pull apart the watercress. She sipped at her wine before she reached for the Boston lettuce, and by the time the cucumber was sliced, the knot in her stomach was relaxing. The smell of pot roast and apple pie rose snugly between her and the drizzling night beyond the cafe curtains.

"Better?" Jenny asked her, and she smiled.

When the pounding began, Jenny reassured her. "It's just Don. He always makes a racket." She called, "Hey, Al!"

But Al was already at the door, and the next moment Professor Young burst in, clutching a paper cone of flowers.

"You'd better start a running program. You're puffing," Al said.

"I had to climb all those stairs. They've roped off the murder area."

They looked at him. He was still trying to catch his breath.

"What murder?" asked Jenny.

"Police all over your lobby," he gasped.

"I don't understand, Don," Al said. "You'll have to put it more clearly."

"A girl was raped and knifed to death." He dropped the flowers and threw himself into a chair, spattering water from his raincoat.

"When did it . . . happen?" Elissa asked him.

"Just now. Fifteen or twenty minutes ago."

"Where?" she whispered.

She looked so distressed, he pulled himself from his own thoughts and focused on her. "In the elevator," he said.

Chapter 5

"Of course, she may have read his body language. Or she might have smelled his fear and aggression," Professor Young was saying.

As dinner had progressed, he had got his wind back. Now his eyes were starting to light and his youthful face was shining with enthusiasm, which made it hard for Elissa to think of him as a real professor. He seemed too young, though Jenny had once told her he was almost forty. "It may have been the tone of his voice, the usual nonverbal stuff," he said.

"She did see sweat on his forehead," agreed Al. "And there was the gesture toward his pocket. That's apt to seem a threat in a stranger."

"But still there's the chance of ESP."

To Elissa they seemed to have spent the whole dinner talking a kind of academic pig Latin. Between the shock of seeing Veronica and her escape from the man in the elevator, she'd only picked at her meal, so that the wine she had drunk had blurred her. As she watched Jenny clear the pot roast from the table, she made a vague try at deciphering the conversation. "What do you mean? What possibility?"

Don turned to her so guiltily she felt he must have forgotten her in his zest for his mysterious subject. "Are you better now? You didn't finish your dinner."

"I'm all right. It's just I wasn't too hungry."

"Sure you don't want to lie down?"

"No, I just wish I could follow what you're saying."

"Oh," he said, surprised that she hadn't understood. "You may have psi talents." And as she still seemed puzzled, "You might be telepathic."

"You mean I read minds?" She couldn't believe he meant it. She glanced toward Al for a hint, but he just looked gravely sympathetic. Then she remembered that Don was a psychology professor and she wondered if it was some kind of experiment. You told people they were telepathic to see how they reacted, whether they just laughed or actually believed it. "But there's no telepathy really. Except in science fiction."

Don looked as if he didn't believe what he was hearing. Then he turned to Al with accusation. "Haven't you told her what you're doing?"

Al seemed embarrassed. "I guess I may not have actually told her."

"But this is the biggest thing of the century! We're turning the whole apple cart upside down. Why should you want to keep it a secret?"

"Come on, Don," said Jenny with a no-nonsense air, "Al's not trying to keep secrets. But Elissa's a friend, not a professional colleague."

"It sounds like you're ashamed, as if we're doing something half-baked."

"Did I say something wrong?" asked Elissa.

"Don's a parapsychologist," Jenny said wryly. "The academic community has made him defensive."

"Now that's unfair!" Don protested. But under the surface sound of outrage his native ebullience was welling up again. "Elissa, I assure you ESP exists."

She nodded unsurely, not wanting to annoy him.

"Now she's humoring me, the sweet creature. Al, try to convince her."

Al leaned across the table, his gentle face serious. "It's true, Elissa. In the past fifteen years there's been a lot of research. The Soviets have twenty-five psi centers for exploring extrasensory talents. NASA is working on psi communication for astronauts. Once we get past Jupiter, it's too far for radio, and telepathy may help. Besides, if we do find intelligent life in outer space, what better way to communicate?"

"The National Institute for Mental Health in Bethesda," Don prompted.

"They've funded studies in telepathy, precognition, and clairvoyance," said Al. "And there are over twelve university laboratories working on it, plus even more research centers. The researchers are physicists, chemists, neurobiologists, psychologists, psychiatrists, physicians making an interdisciplinary attack. The Parapsychological Association has finally been accepted into the Association for the Advancement of Science and physical scientists are starting to look for psychic energy."

"The days of spooks and witches is over," said Don with satisfaction.

"The problem *now* is not whether telepathy is real," said Al, "but what are the best conditions to bring it out."

"Surprised?" Jenny asked Elissa.

Elissa nodded.

"It's partly due to the advance in hardware," Al explained. "The electroencephalograph, biofeedback techniques, Ganzfeld equipment, the plethysmograph—"

"What's that?"

"It measures the blood volume in the fingertips," said

Al. "We tried it on Don while I silently concentrated on a list of names. Some he knew and some he didn't. You should have seen the dial jump when I came to the girls' names."

Elissa glanced at Don, remembering that Jenny had said he'd been twice married. Don smiled at her serenely.

"I'm notoriously susceptible," he said.

She found herself smiling back at the bland admission. "What's Ganzfeld equipment?"

"It blindfolds the subject and cuts off his hearing, which loosens wakeful consciousness. Increases telepathic reception by fifty percent," said Al.

"Don't confuse her with so much detail." Don took over. "To give you a bird's-eye view of the field, Elissa, there's training in biofeedback techniques to improve telepathic abilities. There's research on telepathy between humans and plants—some people *do* have green thumbs—"

"Ingo Swann's experiment with the quark detector," Al suggested.

"Too technical," Don told him. "But the Soviets are even busier than we are. They're working on improving transmission, for instance. When a sender sends an image of a compass, he pricks his finger to make the object more vivid. It does, too. Then there's Vasiliev at the Leningrad Institute who's using long-distance hypnosis to put people to sleep."

"That sounds a bit creepy," said Jenny.

"Possibilities for mischief," Don agreed. And to Elissa: "Are you wondering how it works?"

She wasn't really. She was too confused by the scientific terms and the foreign names, added to the shock of the elevator rapist and Veronica. There was also the wine on an empty stomach. But not wanting to disappoint him, she nodded.

"We don't really know," he confided as if she'd made a telling point. "The Soviet theory is that telepathy functions by low-frequency electromagnetic waves—low-level AC and DC fields. They may be right but we're not sure yet."

He seemed to care so to have her understand that she suddenly wondered why he did care.

"Look at it this way," he said. "The electromagnetic spectrum of what's really out there is a broad band. Your senses just act as filters. What you see with your eyes is only a portion of it. And what you hear with your ears— well, dogs hear sounds that we can't hear."

She asked, "Like dog whistles?"

"Exactly," he said in a pleased way. "But what if our extrasensory system isn't filtered? And we're pretty sure that it isn't. Then we're all constantly receiving telepathic impressions."

"I'm not," she said.

"Don't be so certain," Don told her. "You might be telepathic and not know it. Take dreams, for instance. In dreams some psychiatric patients pick up details from the private lives of their psychiatrists. It's too marked to be coincidence. Freud, Jung, and Fodor all wrote about it. The trouble is, the subconscious masks the messages. It misinterprets or clothes them in symbols. Plus dreams are hard to remember. That's how my own work started— having people remember their dreams. Now I'm developing other psi-favorable states of altered consciousness."

"It sounds interesting," Elissa said, as he seemed so much to want it. It *was* interesting, too, what she understood of it. Still, the uneasy impression lingered that he was trying too hard to persuade her.

"Have you ever shown psi talent?" he asked suddenly.

"Me?" she asked in surprise. "You mean mind read? Never."

"What about tonight?"

She looked toward Al. "You think I was mind reading the man in the elevator?"

Al reached across the table for her hand. "We can't be sure, Elissa. It could just have been his sweating and his reaching for his pocket that upset you. On the other hand, you definitely felt something."

"I didn't feel, I heard voices! A whole weird scene with invisible people!"

"It might have been projection. You picked up his desire to rape you and turned it into voices."

"How do you know it was even the same man who scared Elissa? Had they caught him when you got there?" Jenny asked Don.

"I don't think so. They'd just found the girl's body."

"So maybe it was somebody different, and Elissa's voices were a coincidence."

"In what was it—twenty minutes? Two rapists riding the same elevator?"

"We can't be sure Elissa's man was thinking of rape. He might have been sweating for some other reason. I notice nobody's suggested she talk to the police."

"What could I say?" Elissa asked. "I can't tell them about the voices."

"What if it helped catch him and he confessed?" asked Don.

"If she goes to the cops, they'll take her to the station for a statement," Al said. "She'll be sitting in the precinct house all night."

"Still, if it helped catch him—"

"When did they ever catch somebody from a description? Besides, you have to weigh the stress. The scare she just had in the elevator, plus the trauma last night with Cameron—"

"Al!" Elissa warned.

But Al was looking reflective. "I wonder if seeing him dead—"

"That's not fair! Jenny shouldn't have told you!"

"How could I help it?" Jenny asked. "I was worried about you."

"What's this about seeing somebody dead?" Don asked. "Was it Governor Cameron?"

"It wasn't anybody!" Elissa said desperately.

"Yes it was. Let's see. I know you're one of his staff photographers, so it must have been Steve Cameron. You dreamed he died—no, Al didn't say dreaming, he said *seeing*—"

Al said, "She saw his body lying on a bed."

"Stop, Al. If Elissa doesn't want—" Jenny started.

"It wasn't a dream?" Don interrupted.

"No, she saw him dead in bed. When she came out of the bathroom—" Elissa's eyes flamed bluely and Al stopped.

"Now you've done it," Jenny said.

Al raised his hands in an apologetic gesture. But Don Young said, "Don't be nervous, Elissa. Nobody's making social judgments. We're studying psi potentials, not mating patterns." He turned to Al. "What's your guess? That she picked up his dream?"

"I thought she might have." Al looked pleadingly at Elissa. "Maybe it wasn't fantasy, maybe you really have psi talent. Look, Don's one of the biggest ESP men in this country. He pioneered dream research. His *Telepathy and Dreams* is a textbook."

"Don't bury me under a reputation," Don said, and surprised Elissa by blushing. "Elissa, for thousands of years, people have been having telepathic experiences. Writings are full of it in ancient China, Egypt, and Mesopotamia. About two thousand years ago in India, Patanjali, a great psychologist, described telepathic powers developing during religious meditation. Christian saints often were able to mind read.

"The difficulty is that telepathy is usually spontaneous. It 'just happens' and is all over before anyone can prove it. So in the last century we began applying scientific method. The field work started in the eighteen-eighties when a group of Cambridge professors formed the Psychical Research Society. They collected accounts from people who claimed to have had paranormal experiences, checked them out, and weighed witnesses for reliability.

"I told you about Freud and Jung—how they noticed their patients were picking up pieces of the psychiatrist's life they couldn't have known except by ESP. There were even examples of patients picking up the thoughts and knowledge of *other* patients who shared the same psychiatrist.

"Then in the nineteen twenties, Rhine and Gardner brought ESP into the laboratory. You may have heard about the card tests. After World War Two we began exploring dreams for telepathic cases. We had an agent concentrate, say, on Van Gogh's *Sunflowers* while somebody in another room was sleeping. We woke him up before he forgot what he was dreaming."

Elissa's outrage at Al's betrayal subsided. Her fear that she was following Veronica into madness was so great that any other explanation aroused her hope. "You mean he actually dreamed of sunflowers?" she asked Al.

"Sometimes. Sometimes he did, Elissa. Or gardens, or flowers, or sunshine. It has to come through the conscious filter and it's apt to get distorted. But even if it's not directly on target, with those odds any kind of hit is impressive. After tonight in the elevator—"

"Tonight was suggestive," Don agreed. "I think we ought to test you."

Elissa tried to remember what she knew about Don Young. His casual air confounded her notion of professors. And his bland admission of his susceptibility to girls seemed frivolous. Jenny had once mentioned he was rich, too—he was the heir to a rental car fortune—which made him sound more like a playboy than a serious academician. On the other hand, Al said he had written a well-known textbook. She considered. Perhaps his casual manner was only because he was rich. The Camerons were rich and they were different from other people. A glow seemed to surround them, a kind of radiant sureness. Perhaps the sureness made them better at what they did. Steve was a good Governor; he'd make a good President. And perhaps Don, too, was deceptively excellent. She turned to Jenny and Jenny's smile reassured her.

"Come on," Don said. "Let's go to the lab."

"Tonight?" asked Al.

"I'd like to get right to work on her."

"We could try," said Al, but he sounded doubtful. "She's been upset, though. And we won't have time to teach her the technique."

"We can hypnotize her and get over that hurdle."

Hypnotism had a disturbing ring to it. "What's hypnotism got to do with the testing?"

"We sometimes hypnotize new subjects. It's one way of increasing the psi potential," said Don. "If you turn out to have psi talent, though, we'll want to use another technique. We wire you up to a biofeedback—that's an electroencephalograph machine with a buzzer—and teach you how to slow your brain waves. Just before you start to fall asleep, we buzz you—"

"Let's not prolong the theta state with Elissa," said Al.

"Why not?"

"It's too soon after all the recent stress. The shock about Cameron was only last night. And tonight she was almost murdered—"

"Okay, give her a week to bounce back. There's no history of psychosis?"

As they turned toward her, Elissa felt heat rise to her cheeks.

"We have to be careful," Al told her. "It's a new technique. The best brain waves for telepathic reception are called theta. They're the steady, lowest-frequency waves before you become unconscious. Normally you slide right through them on your way to sleep. But our method keeps you from sleeping, which prolongs the state of theta."

"It's not you, Elissa," said Jenny. "It's the experiment that's uncertain. They don't really know. There hasn't been time to see if prolonging theta is dangerous."

"You make me sound like a mad scientist driving lovely young ladies crazy," Don objected. "And we don't even know if she's telepathic. Okay, tonight we won't use the EEG. Let's just induce a light trance."

"I don't want to be hypnotized," Elissa said firmly.

"It would be sloppy tracking to the lab in the rain," Jenny started.

Don threw up his hands. "Okay! No lab! No hypnosis! An old-fashioned card test here in this apartment."

"Now?" Elissa asked. "You're going to find out if I'm telepathic?"

"Get me the cards, Al," said Don.

Al said, "I don't have Zener cards here."

"Then use playing cards. Let's get started."

"It's not your fault. Everything went wrong with the experiment," Don Young told Elissa kindly. "We couldn't stick you in a different room where you wouldn't be distracted because we didn't have an intercom setup. Besides, I'm a rotten sender. I haven't got a tad of psi talent."

He had just scored her playing card test and she had done no better than chance guessing. Which was worse, she gathered, than if she had scored minus-chance, which might have indicated negative ability.

She told herself she was stupid to have pinned her hopes on being telepathic. But it would have been a better explanation than hallucinations. And she had tried everything Don suggested—shut her eyes, which produced better psi results, and tried to clear her mind before she started. He had the deck of playing cards before him, and as he turned up each card, he'd concentrated on it while she had tried to get a mental picture. She had called it out while he wrote it down. They had let the scoring go till they were finished. But when he'd toted it up, she found the test had been a failure.

She said, "I guess I'm just not psychic."

"I'm not convinced of that yet," Don told her. "We didn't have Ganzfeld equipment to cut out distractions. Besides, cards are intrinsically boring. A lot of fine psi talents won't do card tests. They say they need more emotional context. You know," he said to Al, "we ought to try her on the pictures."

Al turned from the window where he had been watching the rain fall past the panes. "They're in the lab."

"Don uses art prints," explained Jenny. "The agent opens a sealed envelope and takes out an art print. He concentrates on it while a receiver in an isolation room tries to bring in what he's seeing."

Don said, "We can use some other kind of picture."

"Jenny's publisher is bringing out a new art book," said Al.

"That will do it," Don said. He took Elissa's hand and asked, "Not too tired? Aren't you hungry yet? Jenny could fix some sort of a sandwich."

"I'm all right. But since I already failed the card test—"

"Pictures are different. Much more interesting. Come, you'll have to be isolated for this. We'll put you in the bedroom."

"But there's no intercom!" Al objected.

"We're not writing it up. We'll just call out when we start sending. Get a pen and paper," Don told him over his shoulder.

In the bedroom, he sat her on the sleigh bed and arranged the pillows in a mound behind her. "Comfortable? Now I'm going to dim these lights so you can relax," he said, switching off lamps on the bureau and night tables.

"I don't know what I'm supposed to be doing."

"You're going to pick up the pictures we'll be sending.

The three of us will concentrate in the living room. When you get it, you turn on a light and draw it."

"I can't draw."

"Then write down a description."

Al came in and handed her a ball-point pen and a tablet while Don backed off and viewed her with satisfaction. "You *look* full of psi," he said. "If this works, we'll do some real tests with proper hardware. Then we'll train you with the biofeedback."

"Easy, Don," said Al. "She's had a hard night. Don't load her down with too many plans for the future."

"Lie back and relax while we pick out a picture," Don said as they went out, closing the bedroom door.

What did Ganzfeld equipment look like? she wondered, as she lay back in the darkened bedroom. And how would it feel being in biofeedback? Al had mentioned hardware. It had an uncomfortable sound, and she pictured herself trailing wires and plugged into a machine that flashed colored lights. Just the thought of it made her feel trapped.

Besides, the pace of Steve's campaign was picking up. Since their loss in New Hampshire they were increasing the workload before the Iowa and Florida primaries. The number of rallies and fund-raising dinners was growing and the staff photographers were already overworked. She couldn't take time out for complicated testing. Then, too, she couldn't be away without explaining to Steve, and being psychic seemed too peculiar. Particularly after what had happened to his wife. Not that Cathy Cameron's suicide was the same as being psychic, but being psychic sounded unstable. He had two children—he couldn't risk giving them another unstable mother.

Not that Steve was thinking of marriage.

"Okay, Elissa, we're sending!" Don called through the closed door.

Staring into the darkness, she tried to clear her thoughts.

"Don't forget! Close your eyes!" he shouted.

"She didn't have them closed in the elevator," Jenny objected.

"You're right. Do it any way that feels good," he called.

She closed her eyes, opened them again, and tried to decide which was better. She decided on eyes closed. Then she tried to bring in the picture. The trouble was that her mind was a jumble. Red numbers flashed through her brain—a 9, an upside down 7—but that must be wrong. They'd be sending a real picture.

An elephant floated before her. But that was probably a political symbol because of Steve. She thought of a circus. Could it be a circus picture? She saw it clearly: the sawdust-covered ring, clowns, trapeze bars swinging.

Then with a rush, she pictured herself wired into Don's hardware, pointers swinging on dials, lights twinkling, buzzers sounding, and sweat broke out on her forehead. What had Jenny said? "It's too soon to tell if keeping somebody in theta is dangerous." And Don had asked, "Has she a history of psychosis?" Fear swept her.

"How's it coming? Getting anything?" called Don.

She jumped from the bed, found her shoes, and went into the living room. "I can't!" she said, fighting tears. "I don't want to!"

"Come on, Elissa. It takes time. We're not trying to rush you," said Don. "If you want to lie down again, we'll try another picture."

"She's had a bad time. She's getting too tired," Jenny warned.

Elissa stood staring at them sitting together on the sofa above Jenny's book of pictures. They looked at her with concern because they knew about her vision of Steve's death and the man in the elevator. But they didn't know about Veronica's dulled face, her little shuffle in her paper sandals. They didn't know that if they pressed her too far, she might end like Veronica. And she couldn't bring herself to tell them.

Instead she caught up her purse from an armchair,

stepped to the foyer closet, and took out her parka. Before they could stop her, she ran out the door.

Alone in her apartment, she stripped and turned on the shower fixture above her bathtub. For a long while she stood under the spray, trying to wash away the problems that were spinning around her like cobwebs. But the strands were sticky and clung to her. She wished she could call Steve but she didn't know where he was staying and it was only two days before the Massachusetts primary. He was busy turning up at shopping centers, doing television talk shows, giving interviews, racing from one speaking date to another, shaking hands in front of schools, banks, factories, and so on. She wished she knew he hadn't regretted what had happened between them. But he might be afraid she would take it too seriously, fall in love, make scenes, be difficult. Or perhaps he was in love with somebody else. There were hints about Jay Dolan's wife around headquarters. Still, people gossiped; you couldn't believe them. She reached for the shampoo and lathered her hair.

Turning off the shower and wrapping a towel around her, she picked up her hair dryer, sat on the Salvation Army divan, and began blowing her hair dry.

At least she was relieved she hadn't passed Don's card test. It meant he wouldn't be after her to take his lab tests and learn how to bring on peculiar brain states. The necessity had been removed for telling him about the Verricks.

Not that Sam's family was very stable either. She tried to recall what she really knew about the Blakes besides the fact that they had once been gentlemen farmers in Virginia. Well, her great-grandfather, the judge who looked like Edgar Allan Poe, had once fought a duel over a lady's honor and later he'd wagered the last of his hand on a racehorse named Maria. When Maria had lost, he'd drunk himself to death, but it sounded to Elissa as if a man who would bet everything on a horse was already drinking. She knew even less about Sam's father. Except that he had worked on newspapers in New Orleans and San Francisco and Sam had once said he was a morphine addict in the days when you could still buy morphine over the counter. Sam's mother had taken Sam and gone home to Virginia. She had herself died early, Elissa thought, of tuberculosis, and Sam had grown up every which way. So both sides of the family were genetically shaky. Nobody —Blakes or Verricks—ended well. If drugs didn't plague them, it was alcohol or madness. Perhaps the best course for a Blake or Verrick was to die young before the inevitable started happening.

Sitting on the divan, legs folded, she wondered if she had the courage for an early ending. In her despair a wave of homesickness overcame her. Then she remembered that Sam had written he had a phone now. She went to her bureau and rummaged for Sam's last letter. She went back to the divan and called.

When she heard the familiar voice with its trace of Virginia, Sam's tall thin image rose before her. She imagined his bony face and the long, broken nose above the eyes that had seen more than they cared to.

"Hi, dad, it's me. Did I wake you?"

"No. I'm playing backgammon with Delia. She owes me five big ones but she's learning." She pictured them sitting on the top deck of the houseboat over the backgammon board, drinking decaffeinated coffee. When Sam first joined AA, he couldn't sleep because he drank so much coffee, and Delia had put him onto decaf.

"Still campaigning for Cameron?" He continued to maintain his 1960s Tweedledum and Tweedledee opinion of politics. He had taken a lightly sardonic approach to her joining Cameron's staff, figuring she would grow bored and quit quickly. "How's the photography course?"

"Okay. I'm just taking one day a week. And I'm still at Cameron headquarters."

"Thought you might be tired of New York by now and want your room back." When she had left, he'd taken her bunkroom for his office.

"No. I still like it here."

"Well, that's good. So long as you like it." She had a sense that his interest was fraying back to his own life with Delia.

"How's AA?" she asked in desperation.

"I'm still sober," he said laconically.

"How do you like living at the yacht club?"

"Straightsville." He still used the phrases of the 1960s. "Of course, we've got hot showers and it's easier for Delia to get to school now."

"I saw mother," she blurted. She hadn't expected to mention Veronica.

"How did that happen?" he asked with a certain caution.

"I went to see her at Manhattan State."

"How did you know where?" he asked elliptically. He was definitely keeping it vague, obviously not wanting Delia to follow the conversation. She suddenly remembered Delia's quietness the day they'd come upon Veronica's snapshots. Elissa had been unpacking Sam's old suitcase to come to New York and they'd found a stack of old pictures taken at Big Sur. Veronica had been lovely then, slender and laughing, with long hair the same shade as Elissa's. A beautiful vanished wife might have struck Delia as a romantically threatening figure. Perhaps she even feared that a cured Veronica might one day return to claim her husband. "Poor Delia," Elissa thought, and then, "Poor Veronica."

"I looked up Aunt Claudia," she said.

Sam gave a surprised grunt.

"She's working in a movie box office. She wasn't awfully friendly."

"How so?" Clearly now, she realized, he was watching his side of the conversation.

"I don't know. She seemed odd—like she maybe was on something."

He snorted. "She was always pretty cuckoo."

"You mean really? Or just rock star cuckoo? You know, artistic temperament?"

He was silent, suspicious of the question. He didn't like her thinking in terms of family insanity. "Just rock star cuckoo, I guess," he said grudgingly. He hadn't forgiven Claudia for not answering his letters. "So how were things at Manhattan State?"

Coming from Indiana, Delia wouldn't know what Manhattan State was, wouldn't make the connection with her romantic rival. It seemed unfair to Veronica, peering vaguely through the meshed windows, and Elissa had an urge to tell him about the lobotomy, to horrify him into indiscretion.

But the urge dissipated. She reminded herself that Delia wasn't callous, only threatened. Her spinster's world revolved around her idol. And they had put together a workable life. Sam had stopped his drinking and drugging. He was writing again on his stalled novel. And Delia seemed happy enough cooking his meals, fussing, doing his typing. Why should she distress two sober alcoholics? It wasn't even as if they could help Veronica. Nothing could do that now. She decided not to speak of the lobotomy.

Instead she said, "She was quiet. Calm. Much older. Well, I just called to try out your new phone number."

"Imagine me with a phone," he said, deflected. "The old radical is softening." She could hear the pleasure in his self-deprecation. "Sure there's nothing that disturbed you?" he added with a shade of guilt.

"Not a thing," she told him firmly.

"Well," he said, relieved, and she felt his attention begin to stray back to backgammon.

"Night, Daddy. I love you," she said despairingly.

"Love you too, honey," he said and hung up.

As she put down the phone, she told herself it wasn't fair to expect Sam to show concern when she hadn't told him about Veronica. And how could he guess about the man in the elevator or that she had seen Steve Cameron murdered? Yet she'd hoped for some sort of comfort. She was still sitting disconsolately on the divan when the knock came.

She put on a robe, went to the door, and found Jenny, her normally happy squirrel's face shaded with worry.

"Okay to come in?" she asked unsurely. And as Elissa stood back, she entered carrying Elissa's grocery bag. "You left this." Then suddenly she blurted, "I had to come and see how badly we'd upset you. You'd had a terrible time and instead of helping all we did was make things worse."

At Jenny's concern Elissa felt the cold snowball in her stomach melting. It was what she had hoped for from the phone call to Sam but then, not daring to confide in him, hadn't gotten.

"That's okay. I'm just not much good at telepathy."

"You *may* be," Jenny said as if she felt Elissa might take a lack of psi talent as a shortcoming. "I'm not myself though, and I can't say I've been sorry. All those hours wired up to machines while the other kids are out playing." She smiled her hope for forgiveness, and Elissa smiled back weakly.

"I hope you're not mad at Al and Don either. They really can't help it. They get so carried away with the prospect of finding a new psi genius. The implications are enormously important."

Elissa nodded.

"You see, with the physicists coming in, the field is getting very hot now. According to Don, the Space Age is turning into the Psi Age."

"It's all right, really, Jenny," said Elissa, touched by Jenny's efforts to make her understand their excitement. And she was beginning to grasp it dimly—if they could learn how to develop a person's psi talent, it would be like learning how to use electricity, or maybe nuclear energy.

She was still considering when the telephone rang. The thought of Steve shattered her thought and she stepped to the coffee table and caught up the instrument.

"I'm an idiot!" a man's voice shouted. It wasn't Steve; it was Professor Young. "Thank God Al checked the cards again against your scores."

She frowned. "But I failed the card test."

"Only because you were three cards ahead!"

She was silent, not understanding. Jenny looked a question and Elissa shot her a puzzled glance.

"You failed because you weren't calling the cards I was turning up *in the present*," he said. "You were calling the cards I was going to turn up."

She still kept silent.

"Are you there? You hit more than a million-to-one probability. Do you see now? You weren't reading that man's mind in the elevator. You were hearing what was going to happen!"

"Then I wasn't picking up Steve's dream either," she started slowly.

"Not if you're precognitive. You were seeing the future."

"Then that means—" She stopped.

"I'm afraid so."

Her gaze met Jenny's gravely. "Steve is going to be killed," she said.

PART TWO

Chapter 6

Two days later Elissa was standing by the great fireplace at Chadwyck-on-Hudson watching a crowd of Camerons and their friends and advisers celebrating Steve's victory in the Massachusetts primary. Jay Dolan had called that morning to say that Steve wanted her included in the staff car coming up from his New York headquarters.

It was the first time she had seen the Cameron estate. Ever since Tarpon Island she had tried to imagine what it would be like, piecing together bits from shots in newspapers and magazines. But it was even more baronial than she'd expected.

Crystal chandeliers bloomed from the high ceiling; Oriental carpets covered the floor. Eighteenth- and nineteenth-century oil portraits of Mrs. Cameron's ancestors stared down from the oak paneling. The Chinese Chippendale hinted discreetly at family missionaries, old New York judges and divines. It was easy to forget that Old Tom Cameron himself had only moved into New York Republican politics in the vacuum of Hoover's defeat in 1932.

He had supported Landon, Willkie, Dewey, and finally moved to power with Eisenhower. After eight years of state-level success, he emerged as a national figure in 1960 by quarreling with Nixon and making an outrageous switch to the Democrats.

When Kennedy won, he blossomed as a political Merlin. He flourished through Johnson and was briefly obscured during Nixon. But the old magician was only gathering his forces; his sons were growing to an age for public service. Jim was his first hope for President, and when he disappeared in Africa, Old Tom faltered, even renounced future politics. But a year later his upstate machine carried Steve to Albany.

From her place by the fireplace Elissa watched him playing Grand Old Man. The oil stock promoter's eyes were as brightly knowing as ever, the ruddy face glowed with the prospect of fresh battle in Florida, Illinois, and Wisconsin. Even now, in his seventies, he had the sparkle of the invincible lover of women. Elissa remembered that it was he who had installed the secret suite in the museum. And there were rumors that he still engaged in the chase.

Mrs. Cameron, though, was infused with the Dutch virtues. Steadily, doggedly she had held the marriage together during the years when her volatile husband almost demolished it. She had been the ugly spinster daughter of a Dutch Reform minister from an impoverished branch of a distinguished New York family. Fighters of Algonquins and Mohicans, they had held great estates along the Hudson, produced a Revolutionary general, eventually helped to found Columbia University. Their daughters had been marrying Livingstons and Gardners when Vanderbilt was running his ferry from Staten Island. Though their wealth had dwindled, their name was still lustrous as old silver.

And watching Mrs. Cameron working on her needlepoint, Elissa saw that the years had carved the ugliness into distinction. Jim Cameron's death had thinned her

Dutch stockiness; the suicide of Steve's wife had etched her broad face with disciplined pain more intriguing than beauty. She had not lost the straight firmness of her youthful posture. She had greeted Elissa with her old courtesy, asked after Sam Blake, and hoped Steve was not too hard to work for. But before Elissa could answer, Steve's children came downstairs.

They stood flanking their nurse, two bright-faced boys of three and four, in scarlet parkas and snow boots, already recognizably Camerons. The crowd subdued them only briefly. Then they smiled, crowed in answer to Jay Dolan's greeting, and went yelling out of doors. Soon Elissa saw them through the window, joined by two large sheep dogs.

Mrs. Cameron followed Elissa's gaze as the children and dogs vanished behind a stand of fir trees.

"You haven't seen them before? No, of course not. We've never brought them to Tarpon Island. And now with the primaries, we're too busy."

She spoke in the Cameron plural. In the name of politics Old Tom had managed to unite them all in what sometimes seemed to be one creature. In-laws, nephews, nieces, cousins were all campaigning in factories, schools, at fund-raising parties, teas, and luncheons, keeping a fleet of leased planes shuttling back and forth across the country.

"Are they living with you?" Elissa asked.

Mrs. Cameron's eyes hooded in the manner that had developed with Jim Cameron's disappearance and grown more marked with Cathy's suicide. "Steve hasn't the time. Between Albany and these primaries—"

Just then a man appeared at her elbow. "If you can give me those ten minutes—"

"Of course. Please excuse me, Elissa. This is Mr. Newton from *Newsweek*. Let's try the morning room. It will be quieter." She rose and, still carrying her needlepoint, led him away.

It was like that with all of them lately; they were incessantly interrupted. The night with Steve had been a rare occasion, a cancellation in his schedule that happened to fall on her birthday. Her hopes had risen that morning when Jay had told her Steve wanted her to come to Chadwyck, but when she'd arrived, Steve had only given her his usual hug before a dozen people. Then Jay handed him the draft of a speech he was to make during his Illinois swing. Now he was in the library wth more advisers, planning the final lap of the campaign in Florida. She didn't even know if they'd be driving back to the city together, or if he planned to go to Albany. Jay had mentioned an appropriations bill coming up in the State Senate.

As she stood by the fireplace, Elissa saw that the *Newsweek* writer was now talking to Jay Dolan's wife, Amanda. It was the first time that day she'd seen Amanda —when had she come in?—and a corkscrew of apprehension ran through her. That, too, had been happening lately, ever since she'd heard the gossip about Steve and Amanda. It was not really so definite as gossip, simply a quickening of interest, an exchange of glances, an occasional question thrown into a long-distance phone call to Steve's current campaign trip: "Mrs. Dolan aboard at your end?"

There was no reason Amanda shouldn't turn up among the planeloads of celebrities, socialites, and the eastern establishment press who were riding the Cameron bandwagon. Her father's law firm handled Old Tom's Manhattan properties and Mandy had attended the same schools as Jim Cameron's wife, skied the same slopes in Colorado, made the same Easter trips to Bermuda, before her marriage to Jay Dolan.

She and Jay had joined Steve's campaign for Governor, had helped Cathy home from parties when she drank too much, and at her death had joined the family at her funeral. Steve was godfather to the two Dolan children. There was no occasion for more than a question. There was only the radiance of the delicately molded face when Steve joined her group, the too-high laugh when he joked with his advisers, the glance of hazel eyes sketching his hair's outline or lingering on his mouth.

Elissa wondered if Jay had ever asked himself if there was more than that between them. And if he did, would it stir him to jealousy? It was hard to know, seeing the Dolans together. Jay's forces seemed focused on work rather than Amanda. Amanda treated him with an enigmatic lightness that Elissa found disturbing. It might spring from mutual pleasure and amusement. Equally, it might hint at trouble in the marriage.

As the *Newsweek* writer drew Amanda away from the crowd and led her toward the fireplace, it suddenly occurred to Elissa that the museum's secret suite was an unlikely place for a political assassination. How would a strange killer know of its existence? But a friend, say a vengeful husband . . .

The *Newsweek* writer was asking, "Why did she start drinking?"

"Who doesn't drink?" Mandy parried with another question.

"Not like that. Not to end in a sanatorium."

Amanda turned her attention to the fire.

"I've heard stories, too," he said, "about men."

She went on staring at the flames. "Surely now she's dead . . ." she said and trailed off.

"If he makes it to the White House—Presidents aren't private people. Still, the way it's interpreted can be a help. Was it the pressure, do you think, of campaigning?"

The hazel gaze flickered. "I campaign," she said.

"So you do." A cryptic note in his voice. Was it criticism or admiration? "Then you'd say she had some flaw, a basic weakness—"

The lovely head lifted and she saw Elissa. Swinging back to the interviewer, she said, "I can't talk about my friends. You'll have to try someone else who knew her."

As they moved off, Elissa's face burned. Doggedly she went on standing where she was, trying to regain her composure, but now she was self-conscious. She told herself no one had noticed Amanda move off, yet she felt as if the entire room felt that Amanda had led the interviewer away because she'd caught Elissa eavesdropping.

If only Steve or Jay had told her what they wanted in the way of pictures. But in the whirl of Florida and Illinois planning, they had both forgotten her. Then she thought of getting snow shots of the children. Even if they weren't campaign material, Steve would be pleased to have them. When she went to get her coat in the foyer, Old Tom's houseman wasn't there, but she found her parka and boots in the closet and escaped.

The afternoon sun was brilliant, warming the clear air and striking diamonds from the snow-heavy fir boughs. Pulling on her knit cap, Elissa crunched over the ice that covered the arc of gravel driveway and followed a trodden path around a glass-paned greenhouse. She decided it must be a conservatory. She had never seen one before except in old movies on late television. The whole of Chadwyck, in fact, reminded her of the movies, though that might be because she had grown up on a houseboat in the casual, ramshackle Florida Keys.

The house itself was Hudson River Gothic. Stone turrets and tower rooms sprouted from it like mushrooms. Great firs shaded the long approach. Gnarled ivy veined its gray walls. Mrs. Cameron's grandfather had actually lost his Hudson River Valley home before her birth, but Old Tom had bought one even grander with wildcat oil profits in the 1930s. The ancestor portraits had come out of a grand aunt's attic to give the new purchase verisimilitude. Touched now by the Cameron enchantment, the landless years were forgotten; it had become an ancient family demesne.

Following the children's tracks, Elissa found herself crossing what in summer must be the back lawn, past a long swimming pool filled with snowdrifts, and a line of dressing rooms behind an icy hedge of hawthorn. Two blue jays swooped across it, buzzing a squirrel that was stealing seed from a birdhouse, and she stopped to take a picture. Then the sheep dogs started to bark and she continued till the children's tracks vanished on a cleared path. She went more easily then under the snowy branches of elms, beech, and maple, quickening her pace to outstrip recurring thoughts of Amanda Dolan. She had never felt jealousy before and its onset was strange as an exotic fever. Engaged in resisting it, her concentration grew inward, and she came on the river with surprise.

It rolled by the palisade below her, not gray, as it was by the time it passed the factories and reached Manhattan, but slaty-blue, chunked with ice, and very broad. She lingered, watching the powerful current sweeping its ice floes south, then turned to follow the children. The path from the house joined a new path cut into the snow to make a trail along the riverbank. But which direction had they taken? As she stood listening for the cries of playing children, she saw the stranger in a clump of firs.

He was about thirty, with blond, thinning hair and a long, angular face marred by a scar that puckered one eyebrow. His trousers were narrow, sharply creased, and his shoes snow-whitened. He was wearing a leather jacket like the man in the elevator's and perhaps it was the jacket that alarmed her. But when he smiled, her alarm subsided. He said, "I'm just taking a look at the pinecones."

She wondered if he were something to do with the estate, a tree specialist or one of the Cameron gardeners, though his clothes made that seem unlikely.

He rose—he had been sitting on a tree stump—and removed the handkerchief he had been using to protect his trousers. He was tall as Steve, she saw as he refolded the handkerchief and stowed it in his jacket pocket with a gesture so stiffly decorous it relieved her.

"If there's plenty of pinecones, it's going to be a late spring," he continued. "There's other things, of course, besides the pinecones. Woolly bears and the way the moss grows."

He slid his hand into his jacket and produced a silver cigarette case. In the same even way he flicked it open and extended it. When she shook her head, he took one for himself, brought out a silver lighter, and lit it. The gesture called attention to the diamond ring he was wearing, a square bright stone too large to be genuine.

He said, "I'm thinking of buying into the neighborhood."

But there was no neighborhood around Chadwyck. The land about the Camerons was all estates, most too large anymore for private families. Jay Dolan had pointed them out as they'd driven to Steve's place. Some had been willed to religious orders and were now retreat houses, convents, monasteries; a few had become alcoholic sanatoriums.

As if he sensed her doubt, he qualified, "Not one of these big white elephants, of course. A regular house. With an acre or so of property." And then, as if he'd reduced his announcement far enough and was making his stand for respectful attention, "A nice house, though. Two stories, one of those old Victorian places. I'd paint it white with maybe green shutters. And plant a garden with a couple of apple trees."

It had the air of lovingly developed fantasy. But when he added, "I'll fix it up if I have to—I'm handy—and rent out parts for income property," he spoke with practical authority and she was unsure if it was really all fantasy.

But she could not imagine how he had got onto Cameron property. Even if he had come by car, he would have had to park on the public road and walk some distance. Old Tom's driveway had a gatehouse and a caretaker who had recognized the staff car. There were guards who patrolled the grounds as well as the Secret Service men.

"How did you get past the gatehouse? Didn't anybody stop you?" she asked.

"Why should they do that?" he asked with such spurious innocence that she had a feeling that he had spotted guards and evaded them. An ominous thought. And yet, his air of rural frugality still reassured her.

"I think this section is all large estates," she said.

"Is that so?" he asked as if he were receiving surprising intelligence. Then he held his head at an angle as if he were listening, and she realized the dogs had resumed their barking. As the sound grew louder, she guessed that Steve's children had turned back along the river.

"Maybe I'd better try near Nyack." He hesitated as if he were trying to phrase a delicate question. "Are you a friend of the Governor's?"

"I work for him. I'm one of his staff photographers."

He smiled as if her answer pleased him. "Well, I've got to be going along. I have a lot to do. You take it easy now," he told her, turned, and walked away along the river.

Before he stepped from view around the bend, he whirled and shouted: "Hey! Take a message to Cameron. Tell him not to worry. Got that? Say Jack Frost's going to be his friend."

The man who called himself Jack Frost flattened himself behind a spruce until the guard car patrolled slowly out of sight down the highway. Then he ducked down a side road and ran a hundred yards to the red Toyota that was pulled off the road into a screening clump of firs. He unlocked the car, got in, and turning around in the driver's seat, brushed the snow off his shoes, shut the door, and fastened his seat belt carefully. Then, as if nerving himself for an unfamiliar operation, he lit a cigarette, put on his glasses, and stuck the key in the ignition. After a moment, he sat up very straight and pulled out of the firs onto the washboard road.

For the next hour and a half he drove slowly, first along side roads and then on a freeway. He had turned off the heater but despite the cold, by the time he crossed the bridge beside the cars jockeying into Manhattan, sweat pearled his forehead. For half an hour more he made his dogged way through heavy traffic across town, until at last, he pulled into the rent-a-car garage.

At the desk the clerk completed his contract, and he made a show of checking the figures, then slowly signed his name Walter Van Allen. When she gave him his copy, he folded it carefully, tucked it into his wallet, then sauntered into the street.

For a while he strolled, pausing at shop windows as if he were interested in scarves or watches while he checked the passing crowd's reflection. Occasionally he stole glances at his own trim image. At last he pulled back his cuff, exposing a studded leather band, consulted his wristwatch, and whistled softly. Hurrying, he crossed town on Fifty-ninth Street, passing shop windows now without looking, crowding the lights, and winding deftly through the crowds.

At Eighth Avenue, he turned south, strode several blocks past the bus terminal, delicatessens, variety stores, and ducked through a doorway beside a pawnshop. Before him rose a flight of time-scalloped marble stairs.

He took the steps two at a time, swung himself around the iron post of the landing, and, unlocking a metal door, turned on the lights and intently inspected his apartment. But the big seascape reproduction had not been displaced. The standing lamp with its fringed shade was where it should be. The Italian provincial suite was in good order. The glass top of the coffee table shone and its ashtrays were spotless. Bolting the door behind him, he walked through the living room and subjected the kitchen to the same inspection. It was old but the woodwork had been recently enameled. The cafe curtains had been starched and laundered; the towels hanging on their rod were immaculate. Even the gigantic avocado plant on the sill had had its leaves washed.

Crossing the kitchen, he opened the cupboard, took down a baking soda box, and set it on the Formica counter. From his wallet he slid out an American Express card and a plastic-encased driver's license in the name of Walter Van Allen and slipped them inside the baking soda box so they were covered by white powder. Replacing the baking soda, he took down a Wheaties carton and groped in it till he touched a wad of folded money. Replacing the Wheaties, he went into the bedroom.

A poster was spaced precisely equidistant between the twin beds—a smiling, familiar photo bearing the hand-written inscription: *To Jack Frost from his friend Steve Cameron.* As Frost's eye passed across it, he nodded an automatic greeting, then crossed to the closet.

The shirts were hung by color. Shoes were lined up in the shoebag on the back of the door. Trousers were on clip hangers in graded shades from navy to white.

Sliding them along the rack, he exposed a different set of clothes: a tweed jacket patched with leather at the elbows, four cashmere tennis pullovers, a gray suit, jodhpurs, riding boots, a midnight-blue tuxedo. Frost moved a tennis racket in a covered press and unzipped a dustbag. He lifted out a handtowel, unwound it to expose an elegant little 9 mm Luger, then rewrapped it, put it back in the bottom of the dustbag, and rezipped the bag.

Now he began to move more briskly. Tossing fresh clothes on a bed from the closet, he took off his leather jacket and began to dress for work.

By Happy Hour, he was standing in his place behind the bar at Cherry's, mixing drinks for the neighborhood crowd and a few regulars who worked near Fifty-fourth

Street and Sixth Avenue. In his white coat he struck a balance between affable host and efficient technician. He set an old-fashioned on a napkin before a big blonde, put down a bowl of salted peanuts, poured a rye and water for a gray-haired man in a tweed jacket, made change from a twenty, then mixed a vodka martini for a manicurist named Chris.

"Anything new from Walter?" She was about thirty with spectacular breasts, rough skin, and crazy blue eyes. She worked in a beauty salon off Sixth Avenue and was always asking about Van Allen.

"Just that card I told you about from Acapulco," said Jack, smiling sincerely and dropping a toothpick-speared olive in her drink. "When was it? Last week?"

"Did you bring it?"

"I forgot," he said.

"You said you'd bring it."

"I will tomorrow."

"That's what you said last night."

"Well, this time I promise. I'll definitely remember to bring it with me tomorrow."

She plucked out her olive and dreamily regarded it. "I'd really like to see the card. I always liked Walter."

"Walter's all right."

"We were good pals, nothing went on, just kidding around. But we were on the same wave length."

"Yes," he said gravely. "I knew that."

There was a nostalgic silence.

"I still can't understand him living off women. I mean with his education—and he came from a good family."

"He just didn't like work. He used to say he was born to be a playboy."

"Still—living off women."

He sighed. "I guess it's a tough life though."

"A tough life in Acapulco."

He made an ironic noise.

"Remember how he used to sit up like a dog begging?" She smiled. "That was a riot."

"I guess that's the way it is though, taking orders from rich women."

They had this exchange a couple of times a week.

But this time she said, "What I don't get is him running off like that. And then, you know, being gone so long. Over a year now. It's kind of funny."

The scar above his eyebrow twitched. "How do you mean? He ran into this rich woman he used to know and she said 'Let's go to Hawaii.' "

"I thought it was Tahiti."

"Well, whatever. You go to Tahiti by way of Hawaii."

"Still, you'd think he'd call or something, send a postcard."

"He does. He sends postcards."

"I meant to me. I was good pals with Walter."

"She probably keeps him jumping. Going to parties, yachting, like that." His voice was soothing.

She sipped her martini. "Funny, with his manners and gift of gab, ending that way."

"Ending?"

"You know—those women."

He folded and refolded his bar towel. "It was his last shot. He wasn't getting any younger. And what was he— thirty-nine or forty?"

"And broke! I don't know what would have happened to him if you hadn't taken him in."

"I didn't mind," he said. "I have a two-room apartment. He wasn't any trouble."

"Still, it was a damned nice gesture. I'll bet he ended owing you money."

"No. He left all the money he owed on the bureau. The night he packed and left while I was working? I found it on the bureau."

"No kidding! He didn't pay me back my fifty."

"Didn't he? Well, maybe he didn't know your address."

"He could have sent it to me here care of Cherry's. Or to you. If he's sending you postcards, he's got to know your address."

"That's true." He reflected. "I'll bet he just forgot. You know, borrowed it some night when he was drinking and forgot he borrowed it."

"He might have," she admitted. "He sure drank a lot." She pushed her empty glass toward him and he added a dividend from the martini mixer.

"You know, I have a confession. At first I thought you might have thrown him out."

"Me? Throw out Walter? What for?"

"Could be his never having any money. And at first you didn't say anything. It was a while before you told me he'd packed up."

"That's because I thought he might not work things out with his rich lady. If I told you and he came right back, he might have been embarrassed."

"I can see that," she admitted. Suddenly she smiled. "I have a picture of Walter walking in with all his gear— you know, his bags and fancy riding boots and tennis racket. Remember how he was always playing tennis?"

He nodded. "He could only afford to play in Central Park but he said he had to keep his game up the way a violinist had to practice."

Her smile broadened. "He made me laugh. I really miss Walter. I wish he'd walk in right this minute."

"Well, he might."

"Anyway, I'd like to see that postcard."

"I think I've still got it. I don't think I threw it out—" His face sharpened as a tall man entered. "Excuse me," he told her. "I've got to mind the shop."

He went to the end of the bar where the tall man was arranging his long legs around the barstool.

"Hello, Francis. The usual?"

"Let me see now." Francis consulted himself with an

air of gravity. He was a burly, bat-eared Irishman with slow, portentous movements and he was wearing a green guard's uniform. "Of course, it's a damp evening. And I may have a bit of a cold coming."

"How about a whiskey? I could put in hot water and a drop of honey. Up home, for a cold we used honey."

"Still, with guarding the museum and the long night just starting—" He shook his head. "Best stick to the usual." As Jack drew a glass of draft beer and set it on a cardboard coaster before him, he regarded him mournfully. "You didn't come to the Laundromat the way you promised today."

"Yes I did! Where were you? I was there the way we said at three o'clock."

"You said noon!"

"Three. At noon I was painting my kitchen."

"Think of that now," Francis said in amazement. He sipped his beer and put it back on its coaster. "I would have taken my oath on its being noon. I brought you the detergent soap, too."

"I wanted to try that soap," said Jack Frost.

"It's a lovely soap, Sears Detergent. I brought you a jarful."

Jack mopped at the bar and refolded his bar towel. "Well, how are things at the museum? The bigwigs still planning their board meeting?"

"Indeed they are. They'll be coming from all over. Even the Governor. His work permitting. With the warm personal feeling you have for him, I wish you could be getting a look at him."

Jack Frost's angular face began to glow so that the scar above his eyebrow whitened. "Maybe I might. You could say I was your cousin visiting."

"That wouldn't do at all," Francis said, scandalized. "I'm not allowed visitors on guard duty."

"Why not hide me in one of those witch doctor costumes?"

"Holy Mother, the things that you think of!"

"What's wrong, Francis? Think I'm going to snatch him? Or shoot him maybe?" Under Francis's troubled stare, Jack's lips twitched. Finally he yielded to Francis's worry and smiled hugely.

Francis sat back with relief on his barstool. "You oughtn't to joke, the way they're security-minded. Now that he's running for President."

"Have another drink. It's on the house," Jack offered kindly.

Francis inclined his head with dignity. "I accept with pleasure." He tossed off his heeltap of beer.

Chapter 7

Her hopes rose when Steve announced that he would drive
back to the city with them in the staff car.

But while they were loading, Jay Dolan said, "You'll
ride with the Secret Service men, Elissa." The Secret
Service car followed the staff car when Steve was with
them.

Disappointment stabbed her but he had put it so
directly, she could see no way around it. She got in the
back seat of the Secret Service car and two research
assistants piled in beside her.

When Steve came out the front door with Amanda,
they were laughing, and jealousy pricked her. There
was no denying that Amanda looked lovely in blond
mink, and suddenly her own parka felt rough and unbe-
coming.

Steve handed Amanda into the back seat and then
turned and called to Jay, "Where's Elissa?" When Jay
nodded at the Secret Service car, Steve said, "Let's bring
her with us."

Annoyance rippled across Jay's sharp features. "We've got to talk, Steve. The Illinois advance planning—"

"Don't worry, we'll talk. Now go get Elissa."

Jay shrugged but he walked to the Secret Service car, gave Elissa an exasperated look, and said, "You're coming with us."

So after all, she rode into town with Steve. Though he spent the time turned in the front seat discussing staff problems with Jay Dolan.

At least, she thought as they were thrashing out the media budget for California, he was paying her more attention than he was Amanda Dolan, sitting with Jay in the back seat. When he swung back to watch the chauffeur negotiating the freeway traffic, he put his arm about her shoulders. Perhaps, she thought, when they'd dropped off the Dolans and the research assistants and stopped at her apartment, she could ask him in for coffee. Though how she could do it in front of the chauffeur . . . Her face gleamed in the car's darkness. In the end she left it to chance. She leaned back, enjoying the feel of his arm against her. By the time they reached the city, she was drowsing.

"Look at this. She's asleep," Steve was saying, and she returned to full consciousness to see they were in Greenwich Village approaching The New School. He brushed her hair from her forehead in the fond gesture he might have used, it struck her suddenly, for a child or a sheep dog. "Time for class," he said, and she remembered that it was her photography class night.

Pierced by loss, she sat up and made a try at staying with him. "I don't have to go tonight. It's just stuff on light meters."

The limousine slid to a stop at the curb. "None of that," Steve told her. "Up and at 'em."

Amanda reached forward and handed her the knit cap that had slid off while she was sleeping. Tears of frustration came to her eyes. But there was no avoiding class, she saw. Steve was too pleased with himself for remembering that it was her class night. He slid out, gave her his hand, and pulled her to the sidewalk.

"We've got a meeting on this Florida business," he said. "I'll ring you at home when it's over."

It happened so fast, she didn't remember later if she had even answered. She was certain, though, she smiled. She had a sense of relief and joy and radiance. Then he stepped back into the car and it drove off.

She entered The New School, still smiling at the knowledge that he hadn't forgotten, that he had even adeptly planned to see her later. Brushing past other students, she ran up the stairs to her class.

A note was tacked to the door saying that that night's class was canceled.

Standing in the crowded hallway, she tried to decide how to make the time pass until his phone call. She supposed she could drop in on Jenny and Al. If they weren't home, she might develop the day's negatives in the darkroom she had set up in her closet. Then if he came by that night, he could see the contact prints on the shots she had taken of his children. And that reminded her of the encounter with Jack Frost. She must tell Steve that she had met a stranger on the grounds at Chadwyck. The Secret Service or Old Tom's private guards should have prevented it. With so many kidnappings and assassinations— As the thought struck her, she stood quite still in the crowded hallway, trying to bring back a clear image of the boyish face, the puckered scar, the ingenuous air, and her conviction that he was lying. He could have been carrying a gun under his jacket.

But when she'd seen Steve killed, it had not been at Chadwyck. It had been at the museum.

"Aren't you Veronica Verrick's daughter?"

Startled, Elissa turned to confront a woman with the eyes of a Mexican magician. She looked Latin—Spanish perhaps. She was wearing jeans and a denim workshirt but her black hair was streaked with gray and her age was indeterminate; she might be fifty or she might be seventy. "Are you?" she pressed. And as Elissa nodded, she extended a muscular, paint-spattered hand. "I'm Valdez."

Elissa knew the name from The New School catalogue. Her thumbnail biography said she had been a student of Orozco, had exhibited in Mexico, Paris, and the New York Museum of Modern Art, and was teaching a course in mural painting.

"I knew your mother," Valdez said. "You look just like her." The magician's gaze wavered, revealing another Valdez, curiously unsure, almost humble. "In fact," she started, then stopped as if words were not her normal language. "I've seen you before," she admitted awkwardly. "When I first saw the resemblance, I followed you home and checked the apartment mailboxes. You're Blake?" and as Elissa nodded, "Veronica married a Blake."

She seemed not to know who Sam Blake was. Elissa had met other painters, friends of Sam's, who lived in a world of paint, canvas, and gallery intrigue. They didn't read much.

"How is she?" Valdez asked. And as Elissa hesitated to admit to Veronica's condition, "I sometimes see Claudia but she's so strung out—"

"She's in Manhattan State. I saw her last weekend." Elissa paused. "I'm not even sure she knew me."

Pain crossed the mobile face. "How about a drink? My place is nearby."

Elissa hesitated. The black magician's eyes, the jeans, the muscular fingers clawing the short, streaked haircut made her uneasy.

But Valdez said, "Please come," in such a homely, humble way, her nervousness evaporated. They went together down the staircase and through the school entrance into the cold March night.

The ice that had melted during the afternoon was starting to harden. It glimmered under the street lights and they walked slowly, picking their way across the slippery patches. A chill mist was blurring the car lights, veiling the city grime and softening the outlines of the hotels and apartment houses along lower Fifth Avenue. For a few blocks Valdez was silent.

Then as they turned the corner, she said, "I was your age when I first saw this. Fresh from a little border town in Texas."

They gazed at the neon signs, the shops, and crowds of young people thronging Eighth Street. Harpsichord music showered them from a record shop. A sky-blue paper carp floated from a Japanese store.

"In those days there were gods in the Village," Valdez said as they wove their way between two fruit stands piled with green and purple grapes. In the fruit store she purchased a bag of red apples. "Eugene O'Neill, and Edna St. Vincent Millay. The Provincetown Players started over there on MacDougal," she continued as they left and wandered again down Eighth Street. "Have you ever heard of Aleister Crowley?" And as Elissa shook her head, "He was a sorcerer really. He lived over there in a basement apartment. They called him the wickedest man in the world."

An invisible Greenwich Village seemed to rise and shimmer in the mist about them. Elissa herself could not see it but she felt it was there for Valdez, and she was quiet, not wanting to dispel a world of poets and playwrights long vanished. Then Valdez sighed and led the way through a door set into the brick wall beside a leather shop. They climbed a flight of dimly lit stairs and Valdez pulled a key ring from her jeans, turned two locks, and swung it inward. "They say I should move but I've had it for over thirty years. Anyway, I'm mostly in Mexico or Paris."

Valdez, for all her wiry darkness, must be over seventy, Elissa decided as she stepped past the thick steel door.

The great studio room was alive with paintings. They hung on the walls, boldly structured in vibrant reds and blacks and whites: phalanxes of Zapata's soldiers, the pure lines of an ox skull illuminated by noon radiance, the fluid shapes of peons working in geometric hemp fields.

As Elissa stood dazzled by color and power, a Siamese cat leapt from a ledge of plants to Valdez's shoulder; a large black male, tail in the air, strolled to her.

"This is Beauty," she said, stroking the Siamese. "The Beast is her son. One night I forgot and left the windows open."

With Beauty riding her shoulder and Beast complaining at her heels, she led the way over Navaho rugs to a Pullman kitchen. After feeding the cats she filled a tray with wine, cheese, and the apples that she'd just brought from the fruit stand, then carried the tray to a low oak table set before a leather divan.

"Come! Children are always hungry," she said with curious harshness. But as Elissa sat tentatively on the edge of the divan, she sighed again as if the harshness were not able to contain her deeper sadness. "Elinor Verrick was my first friend in the Village. For years she was my best friend. It's hard to believe she's dead, it's gone—" She lifted a strong hand and let it fall in a submissive gesture. "She was a great woman, your grandmother, a brilliant, beautiful woman like fire, like flame."

She poured out Burgundy and passed Elissa a wineglass, but Elissa held it thoughtfully, not drinking. Her own picture of her grandmother, pieced together over the years from Sam, had been of a wild woman, half-crazy, often drunk, taking dictation on a planchette from spirits.

"Didn't she drink?" she asked Valdez.

"Not till later when she lost Owen." Owen was Elinor's second lover, Veronica's father. "She was slender, with long auburn hair. Her skin was luminous as pearl in some lights. And her talk was delicate, complex, I can't describe it. They don't speak like that anymore—it made me think of nightingales."

"Was it true about Lord Byron?"

Valdez nodded sadly. "Later. Much later. I myself used to take down the messages." The dark, stern face grew inward. "What else could I do? I loved her."

Elissa was silent, respecting the pain of the disciplined old woman.

Then the lines of Valdez's face softened. "But in the beginning, when she lived on Bethune Street— It was an old Federal house with sunflowers in the front yard. Revelers used to carry them off at night." She suddenly smiled. "She kept white cats and white rabbits—they had the run of the house—"

"Why rabbits?"

"I don't know. She liked them. But the effect—you'd look up and see a huge white rabbit—" She shook her head. "It doesn't tell you—former times are like some wines, they don't travel."

Elissa smiled. "I think I understand about the rabbits."

"Do you?" Valdez asked, her fine face lighting. "Those two men, handsome, arrogant, one after the other, like bold princes. And the children. Claudia, brave and auburn-haired like her mother. Veronica, thin, with delicate bones and hair like Owen's that shone about her like an aura. I remember the girls playing hopscotch— Come, I'll show you!"

She rose and led Elissa to a small cell-like bedroom. There was only a single bed in it and a polished oak dresser. Over the bed hung a painting. The line was misty and romantic, unlike the oils on view in the studio. Two wraithlike children in white dresses were playing hopscotch. The chalk marks in the dusk looked arcane, like magic diagrams.

"I call it *The Witch's Children*," said Valdez. "The Museum of Modern Art wants it, but I can't sell it. I've promised to leave it to them when I die."

Elissa was silent, fearing to break the conjuration of the summer twilight, the chalked pavement, the suggestion of darting, hopping children.

"Veronica was unearthly," said Valdez. "She was psychic. She saw things we couldn't see, like a cat does."

Elissa's brows contracted and Valdez read the movement as disapproval. "She saw things," she repeated stubbornly. "Once it was an old man in a nightshirt, choking. My father died that night. In Texas. Of throat cancer. And once she screamed at Owen that his head was bloody. She wouldn't stop—she screamed and screamed."

Elissa's grandfather, Owen, she remembered, was beaten to death by blows on the head.

When she left Valdez's studio an hour later, she found that the mist had thickened. Girls huddled in coats and parkas passed her on Eighth Street and it seemed to her they were all hurrying to meet lovers, husbands, families. Steve hadn't foreseen that her photography class would be canceled and wouldn't expect her home till later. The thought of a long wait for his phone call made her delay returning to her apartment. To kill time she stopped and inspected a bookshop window.

It was already nine o'clock but the crowds were still moving sluggishly between the tables piled with paperbacks. She had almost decided to go in and see if they had books on seeing the future, when a staring face materialized before her on the windowpane. Its lips moved. "Veronica!" it whispered.

She felt as if she were going down too fast in a skyscraper elevator. Whirling, she found that the face was Claudia's reflection.

She was wearing a pale, soiled cape and rubber rainboots. The champagne-colored hair had come out of curl and hung dankly about her shoulders. The vein in her temple had swollen; her raw, roughened skin was tight with anger.

"Veronica, what are you doing here? You promised you'd take care of mother!"

"It's me, Aunt Claudia. It's Elissa," she protested. But the blue saucer eyes flashed and Elissa knew she hadn't heard.

"You know how bad she is today. She's drinking *brandy*," Claudia hissed. "I'll bet you're out here to meet some boy."

Oh God, Elissa thought, realizing that Claudia was seeing another time, another world. In that world Veronica, lovely and ever-young, had slipped out to meet some love, leaving their mother dangerously alone.

"Aunt Claudia, listen. Elinor is dead. Veronica is . . . gone. I'm Veronica's daughter," Elissa said, trying to put authority into her voice. "I saw Valdez and she told me that Veronica was psychic. Is it true? Do you remember?"

But Claudia repeated stubbornly, "You're just trying to get out of helping mother. Go ahead, then! Wait for your boyfriend. I'll tell mother how you left, and she'll hate you!" Her raw face fiery, the blue eyes shining with malice, she turned and plodded away in her rubber boots.

Elissa watched until the pale rain cape was swallowed by the crowds and mist. She had a sense of being a ghost from a time long vanished. Turning resolutely into the bookshop, she purchased a paperback and headed home through Washington Square.

She walked beneath the arch and went along the path toward the fountain, dry and empty now in winter. The trees were bare and patches of pocked snow gleamed from the darkness. The stone chessboards had no players. A trio of winos called to her from a bench but she didn't look toward them and their interest faded as a policeman sauntered by her.

Gradually Valdez's words began to drift through her

distress about Claudia. She thought of Veronica and Claudia as children, imagined them playing children's games on the chalked sidewalk before the old house that had so long ago passed out of the family. She wondered which number it was on Bethune Street and wished she had asked Valdez. Then she could see where her grandmother had raised her witch's children. But soon the pictures became unstable. The hopscotching children began to waver, melt, and run into their terrible futures: Claudia crazily reflected in the bookshop window, a frail, aging Veronica smiling vaguely through meshed windows. What exactly was it Valdez had said? "She was psychic. She saw things."

Digging her hands deep into her parka pockets, Elissa tried to recall if Veronica had been psychic during her, Elissa's, childhood. Certainly Sam Blake had never said so. Though, of course, Sam disliked the occult, in fact was militantly rational. From her own memory she tried to recall signs of precognition, of what Professor Young and Al Martin called psi talent. But as soon as she opened the door to her own childhood, horrors began tumbling out: Veronica's desperate hands beating on windows, Veronica screaming that evil insects were flying across the water toward her.

She shook her head to blot out the pictures, and as she tried to focus on the present world around her, a dark bundle at eye level caught her attention. She couldn't identify it, and trying to make it out more clearly, she moved closer.

It was a black man, his eyes and tongue dreadfully protruding, clothes stained by his last agony, dangling from the tree where he'd been hanged.

In her shock her senses failed her. She tried to cry out but no sound came. She stood frozen.

Then a great clanging filled the dark air around her. She heard glass smashing and the screams of frightened women. Puffs of flame and crimson smoke billowed from the brownstone houses. The street lights were gone but by the red glare that ringed the horizon, she saw men laying axes to a telegraph pole on MacDougal Street. A crowd was hurling bricks at the house windows.

With tremendous effort, she pulled herself from the languor that overwhelmed her. She tried to confront the sudden confusion; she tried to think. Was there a chance, she wondered, they were shooting a movie?

The men were in costume. Their trousers didn't seem right and there was something odd about their collars. One man had a Bowie knife; another carried an old musket. But there was no sound truck; there were no spotlights, no snaking cables. And the sense of real danger was thick around her. She stole another look at the hanged man. From the angle of his head, she knew his neck was broken. Nausea rose in her throat.

Then she saw the tree above him was in leaf.

She turned, feeling her legs tremble under her. All the trees in the park were in full leaf. It was summer.

As a mob rounded the corner, lighting the night with torches, terror suddenly released her from paralysis. Screaming, she fled into MacDougal Street before them.

Suddenly brakes screeched. Her vision blurred and she went down.

"Elissa!"

Pain stabbed her hands and she was dragged back and righted on the pavement. Groggily, she looked about at Professor Young's concerned face, saw a panel truck with an angry driver.

As the truck sped on, Professor Young put his arm about her. "Are you okay? Scratched your hands up but there doesn't seem to be any serious damage."

She glanced at her palms, scraped where she had broken her fall on the paving. A bruised vein in one wrist was swelling. But the mob with the torches was gone. The clanging had stopped and the street lights were back in the normal way. She turned to Washington Square but there were no fires, no smoke, no glare on the horizon.

She searched for the black man but the awful bundle dangling from the tree had vanished. The trees themselves were bare of leaves. The whole park was bare now. Patches of snow gleamed again from the darkness; it was still winter.

"The black man. He was hanging. I think they'd lynched him." She stopped in confusion.

He studied her carefully. She was afraid he was going to lecture her about running in front of panel trucks. But instead he said with decision, "You'd better come along with me."

"You were crossing Washington Square when you saw him?" Don prompted at the coffeehouse table.

She had cleaned her scraped palms and the waitress had brought an ice cube from the kitchen to hold against the vein in her wrist. But terror was still washing over her. The past few days seemed like a cargo broken loose in a gale-tossed ship. She looked at a Renaissance courtier painted on the wall and she was back viewing Steve's blood-soaked body. The Vivaldi on the coffeehouse stereo was filled with the rapist's murmurings. She kept getting afterimages of Veronica's blank face.

"The hanged man—he was black?" Don asked her.

As she nodded, the boy with him bent forward intently. He was in his late teens and so thin that the bones showed beneath his shaved skull. Don had introduced him simply as Billy, and added, "He's working in our ESP experiments."

"Tell me exactly what you remember," Don said.

She made another attempt to sort out what had happened at Washington Square.

"Well, there were fires in the houses and a mob with torches. Men were cutting down a pole on MacDougal. They were strange—"

"Telegraph pole?" And when she nodded, "How were they strange?"

"There was something funny about their collars. And one man had an old musket. I thought maybe they were shooting a movie." She paused. "But the worst part was the leaves—it was summer."

"Summer," Don said with barely suppressed excitement. "How did you see so much? How was it lighted?"

"The fires. And later the mob came around the corner with torches. Besides, there was a red light on the horizon. Sort of a glow as if—" She stopped unsurely.

"As if there were fires all over the city?"

"I know it sounds crazy. Maybe I'm going crazy like Veronica."

He stopped her with an impatient gesture. "Did you hear what people were saying?"

She shook her head. "It was hard to make out over all that shouting. And the women screaming."

"What women?"

"I didn't actually see them. I guess they were inside the houses where the men were smashing the windows. And then with all the clanging—"

"What was clanging?"

"I don't know."

"Maybe fire bells?"

"But they *rang*."

"They didn't have sirens a hundred years ago. They had bells mounted on horse-drawn fire trucks."

Dismay struck her speechless. She stared at him.

"Actually more than a hundred years ago," he told her. "In the summer of eighteen sixty-three. Washington Square during the Civil War draft riots. Well, think what you told me. Fires all over the city, torches, vandals. A black man lynched from a tree."

"In New York?" asked Billy.

"The Civil War was unpopular in the city. Even the

Mayor wanted to secede from the Union. When the draft started, there were riots. The police commissioner was stomped to death. The draft offices were burned and the telegraph wires cut. After the mobs looted the liquor shops, they got drunk and tried to burn the town down. Blacks were hung. The government had to bring back troops from Gettysburg." He looked at Elissa closely. "You hadn't read about it?"

She shook her head in mute misery.

"Don't look so unhappy," said Don. "You're not the first in the world to have it happen. Some people do see the past. One woman who was walking through the gardens at Versailles found herself back in the seventeenth century. And there's the famous Dieppe case. Two Englishwomen in a Dieppe hotel heard the sound of bombing. There was gunfire and shouting. But when they asked, nobody else had heard it. So they reported it to the Society for Psychical Research. The PRS checked their story against unpublished War Office records and found the timing of the sounds paralleled the bombardment and landings of the Dieppe raid on the beach below their hotel during World War Two."

Billy sat up straight, his thin face tense with excitement.

"It's well documented," Don said. "The thing is, Elissa, you seem to go both ways. You see the past and also the future—the draft riots, the man in the elevator, and Steve Cameron—"

"Governor Cameron?" asked Billy. Elissa shot Don an anguished look.

"That's classified," he said. "You seem to be slipping around in time," he told Elissa.

"But that's impossible! I mean, you can't really see into the future."

"Precognition has a long, honorable history. The Delphic oracle predicted the future for Greek kings and heroes. In the Bible there's Pharaoh's dream about the fat years and the lean years that came to pass. You have Nebuchadnezzar's precognitive dreams in the Book of Daniel. And King Belshazzar's vision, which was visual and detailed as yours are. In the New Testament, Joseph fled into Egypt because of a dream. Christ himself prophesied at the Last Supper, remember? That Peter would deny him. In medieval times there was Nostradamus. And in recent years, there's been Cayce, Eileen Garrett, Arthur Ford, Gerard Croiset, Jeanne Dixon—"

"I still don't see how it could happen. If it's already *there*, laid out, before we get to it—" Her mind seemed to cloud before she could finish the sentence. Her wrist began to throb again and she put her other hand beneath the table to hold it.

"It's there all right," Don told her. "It's just that our modern world view is based on linear thinking. We see events as happening in sequence. So it seems impossible. But other peoples view it differently. Oriental philosophies have always held that a part of the universe lies beyond that sort of logic. And now parapsychology agrees with them. So does advanced quantum physics. And electrical engineering. When electrons move in an electromagnetic field—"

"She might not be up on her electrical engineering." Billy grinned and Elissa gave him a wan smile of gratitude.

"Have you ever heard of the Aberfan disaster?" Don asked, and as she was silent, he said, "It happened in Wales in nineteen sixty-six. Mine slag slid down a mountain and covered a schoolhouse. It killed more than a hundred children. There were thirty-five *recorded* predictions."

"I like Cox's railroad accidents," Billy prompted.

"Okay. Cox investigated twenty-eight United States railroad accidents. He found there were statistically fewer passengers on accident days than just before or just after the accidents. Which looks like people had precognitions or just plain hunches. They didn't take the railroad that day."

"But how does it work? What makes it happen?" asked Elissa.

"Nobody knows. That's one of the things we're investigating. I could give you a lot of theories—Professor Good thinks we may send ourselves telepathic signals that circle the universe. The signals come back like an echo. Dunne thought that in some states of mind, we see from a point in infinity. Wasserman felt that psi fields send advance information as copies that travel back faster than the originals."

She gave up following the theories. They didn't seem to be sure of anything. "But why me?" she asked.

"Well, since our senses filter out most of the impressions from the world around us, I'd guess your filters have become defective."

"What would make that happen?"

"Sometimes accidents—a hit on the head—seem to start up ESP. Sometimes hallucinogenic drugs."

"I haven't been hit on the head. And I've never taken mescaline or LSD."

"Then it might be genetic." Suddenly he asked, "Who's Veronica?"

She felt a rush of blood flood her cheeks.

"I'm not psychic," he assured her. "You told me yourself. A while back while you were telling me about the draft riots. You said, 'Maybe I'm going crazy. Like Veronica.' Who's that? A friend? Or a relative?"

"My mother," she whispered.

"Is she dead?" She shook her head. "What's wrong with her, Elissa?"

"She's in Manhattan State Hospital. She's had a lobotomy."

"My God." Pain crossed his face. "They don't even know what psychosis is yet. So they cut."

Elissa was struck by the bitterness. After a moment Billy tried to explain. "You see, they're starting to think that maybe all psychotics aren't really crazy. They might be psychic. Like maybe they really do hear voices. Not actual voices, but they pick up the thoughts of people around them." He hesitated. "I was in Rockland State Hospital myself. I kept hearing these really weird things, but it turned out I'm psi. I'm a telepath. Don tested and found out I was picking up my brother's thoughts. He's a science fiction buff and I was getting the stuff he was reading."

Elissa's mouth grew dry. "You mean they'd put people away in asylums who are really telepathic?"

"Not on purpose, of course. The doctors think they're psychotic."

"But do you think that often happens?"

"Yes," Billy said. "Very often. It sure happened to me."

Feeling sick, Elissa thought of Veronica. She remembered what Valdez had said about two little girls hopping over chalk marks in the dusk, "the witch's children." She heard Valdez say, "She was unearthly. She saw things."

"She saw things," she repeated.

"What did she see?" Don asked her.

"Insects. Flying toward her. They crawled in her ears and she kept spitting, trying to spit them out."

Don's gaze sharpened. "Is that what she called them? Insects?"

"Evil insects. She said they were invading her brain."

"Was anyone around her sick?" And as she shook her head, "Nobody at all? Sure? Sisters? Brothers? With some brain illness like encephalitis? Meningitis? Cancer?"

"I'm an only child. Her sister's still alive. She had no brothers. There was only her sister and her mother." She stopped. "My grandmother, Elinor Verrick. She died a year later. Of cancer. Brain cancer."

There was a long, terrible silence.

"Did your mother have any previous psi experience?" asked Don finally.

"She . . . saw a man the night he died in Texas. She was in Greenwich Village. Then she saw a man with a bloody head. He was beaten to death later." She imagined Veronica's vague face, the restless blue eyes. The thought of mental hospitals filled with psychic talents made her weak. She took a deep breath. "Can we do anything?"

"You can take the psi tests, learn to bring on other visions."

"But about her? She's had a lobotomy. Is it too late?"

He didn't answer directly. He just said, "I'm sorry. But for Cameron—" He glanced toward Billy. "If you could pick up more of the circumstances, how it happens, who's going to do it. Maybe we can stop it happening."

"Can you do that?" Billy asked. "I mean, if it's already in the future—"

"Sometimes," Don said.

"Louisa Rhine says only nine cases in a hundred and ninety were prevented."

"Nine is sometimes," Don said firmly, and turned to Elissa. "How about it? You've had three visions in a few days now. That makes you top priority. You're the best we have to work with. Do you want to use your talent to stop something happening to Cameron?"

She still felt light-headed from the shock of the visions. And the new knowledge that Veronica had been seeing Elinor's future invasion by cancer when Sam wrestled her into the skiff and the patrol car drove her to the hospital. Then the terrible round of hospitals, ending finally in lobotomy. When she thought of it, horror almost overwhelmed her.

But if there was a chance to stop Steve from being killed, she knew she would have to try to look once more into the future.

Forcing herself to move, she nodded.

"We'll fit it in around your working schedule. We'll start tomorrow night," Don said.

She was home before nine. But by eleven Steve still hadn't phoned her. She didn't shower because she was afraid that with the water running, she'd miss his call, and to help pass the time, she worked in her closet darkroom. The swollen vein in her wrist had returned almost to normal, but her scraped palms stung and made her clumsy developing the pictures. Still, the shots of Steve's sons in the snow came out well and she stood for a while gazing with a magnifying glass at the contact sheet.

Four-year-old Tom, Jr., had Steve's long slender lines and the hawky Cameron look. But three-year-old Pete was still encased in baby chub. It seemed to her, though, that he had the quiet, almost sad expression she'd seen in newspaper pictures of Cathy.

She tried to recall if she'd noticed the look when she'd first seen Cathy's photos in the newspapers after she and Steve were married, or whether it only seemed so after Cathy had slashed her throat. Had tragedy been mirrored in her gaze so early? If the future were seeable, then wasn't it *there* somewhere, lying in wait? Might some dim general consciousness come back like an echo? She tried to remember what Don had said about psi fields sending copies that traveled back faster than their originals. But as she seemed to verge on understanding, it eluded her.

She returned to studying Pete's photos and it seemed to her there *was* a strange quality about them. Still, it was more likely he simply reflected the tragedy that had already happened, the missing mother he couldn't quite remember, the hesitation when her name was mentioned. It didn't have to be a future tragedy waiting for his father.

The telephone rang and she dropped the pictures.

At the sound of Steve's voice joy flooded her. He hadn't forgotten; he'd promised to call and he had remembered.

"Sorry," he said. "Florida was a worse mess than I expected. Were you asleep?"

"No!" She nearly shouted, hoping maybe he'd still come over. Then, confused because she'd shown her joy so clearly, she added, "I've been developing pictures. I got

some good ones today of the children." He didn't speak
at once and she forced herself to boldness. "Did you want
to come over?"

"Tonight?" His surprise sent a wave of shame through
her. "I've got to be up at five tomorrow. We're going to
Chicago."

She made a quick sound of agreement.

"Listen, Elissa, Carl's sick. He's got the flu." It took her
a moment to place Carl, a square-faced young man with
a brash manner, one of the tour photographers.

"How about it?" He added, "We'll be on the road for
ten days—Illinois, then we go to Florida. Want to come?"

"You mean leave tomorrow?" she asked, suddenly remembering Professor Young and his psi tests. If they
missed a chance to stop Steve's future death, mightn't the
future arrive before they had another chance to stop it?

"Okay?"

She wanted to say, "It's not okay! I saw you dead!"
And yet, of course, she couldn't. He'd think she was
drunk, stoned, going crazy.

"Elissa?"

"Oh. Okay."

"Be ready at six. I'll pick you up on the way to the
airport."

If they could only talk. By tomorrow there'd be so
many interruptions. "Steve," she started, gathering her
courage.

But he said, "Go to bed, hon. See you tomorrow," and
hung up.

Chapter 8

Ossipee, N.H.
March 2

Dear Grandson Jackie,

I hope this finds you well and getting along in New York City. Do you still have the job in that bar? I wish you didnt have to work around likker. It is a terribel temtation for some. (I thank the Good Lord you dont have this weekness.)

Its snowed heavy this winter—8 more inchs this week. And cold too. 20 below when I got up at 5. I heer theirs 3 feet of ice on the Lake. Still cant see the road from my house but dont you worry your Aunt Duck has been doing my shopping. Shes easier to take now that The Change is over—she dont talk so much and dont loose her temper so bad either. I dont know how your Uncle Jed used to stand her. But she says she didnt run off like your mother anyway. Do you guess she ever made it to California (your mother?). Its 20 years now she could be dead. Well the tares will be gathered and burned in the fire. Matt 13:40

Your cousin Jim shoveled a path so I can get to the henhouse.

Rev. Johnson had flu and ended up almost dying spent two weeks in the hospital but is on the mend now. Poor old Mrs. Bowen had another stroke and she dont no her own family.

Those snowmobilers wold drive a saint to drink. 2 nights ago they cut across my backyard but Frisky barked himself crazy and it scared them off. Am pretty sure it was those Zambreskys.

Not but you weren't wrong doing that to Pete Zambresky. He still cant move his legs and I heer hes doped up all the time now. I warned you not to get clos with that Pete. Them Zambreskys have bad blood and it dont excuse you that he picked up a rock to fight with. They could of sent you away for that tire iron. Do you still get bad headaches? I hope not. Pray to God, Jackie to help control your temper. I hope your still going to church.

Yours loving Grandma

P.S. I had a flareup with my arthritis but been using honey and am getting around pretty good for 84. Thanks for sending the money at Christmas. Did you get the fruit cake?

Jack Frost finished reading the ruled pages standing at the mailboxes in the vestibule. Suddenly his puckered eyebrow began to twitch and he raised his hand to stroke it. He stood for several minutes, stroking, then turned abruptly and carried the letter and a bill up the stairs.

In his apartment he took off his glasses and walked around the living room in agitation until his attention finally fixed on the seascape and he straightened its gilt frame. Next he spotted a cigarette ash in an ashtray and removed it.

Gradually his eyebrow quit twitching. Still wearing his

leather jacket, he replaced his glasses and opened the bill addressed to Walter Van Allen. It was from American Express for annual dues. Enclosed flyers offered a wristwatch, a vacation in Spain, and a cassette player. He examined the advertisements with care before he threw them into the wastepaper basket. Then he stuck the bill and the return envelope into his wallet and replaced the wallet in his hip pocket. His grandmother's letter he carried into the bedroom and slid beneath his rolled socks in his bureau. Finally he went back through the living room into the kitchen.

He fished a fifty-dollar bill from the Wheaties box in the cupboard and tucked it into his wallet with the American Express bill. Then he walked straight out of his apartment, double-locking the metal door as he left.

A pale morning sun shone wanly through the smog above Eighth Avenue as he strode through the crowds coming out of the bus terminal. Seeing an old lady attempting to lift a suitcase into a taxi, he suddenly stopped and swung it into the back seat for her. When she thanked him, a fresh, boyish smile illuminated his face.

Two blocks farther on he entered a bank, bought a twenty-five-dollar money order, and took it to a counter where he made it out to American Express and signed Walter Van Allen's name. He slid both bill and money order into the return envelope and went to a stamp machine. Outside, he dropped it into a mailbox. Then he consulted his stud-banded wristwatch and hurried into a market down the street.

At one o'clock Jack Frost, with a spotless towel about his waist, stood at his kitchen sink arranging two luncheon plates of cold ham and sliced tomatoes. Adding potato salad from a pint container, he slipped the plates into the refrigerator to chill. Then he emptied a polyethylene bag of rolls into a cake pan, set them on the stove, and began to warm the oven. Finally he strolled to the doorway and surveyed his living room.

A cut glass decanter, newly filled with whiskey, stood with an ice bucket and two shining glasses on a tray atop the coffee table. Woven mats and napkins lay on the Italian provincial occasional table. All was orderly, dusted, ready. Five minutes later the downstairs doorbell rang.

Pressing the answering button, he picked up the ice bucket and hurried to the kitchen. When he returned with ice, his own doorbell was ringing. He inspected his guest through the peephole, then turned the locks in the metal door, and swung the door open.

"Have I found the right place now?" asked Francis jovially, extending a gift-wrapped package the size and shape of a liquor bottle.

"You didn't need to do that," said Jack, accepting it and setting it on the coffee table. "Come in."

Francis removed his green guard's cap as he stepped across the threshold. "I hope you don't mind me wearing my uniform. 'Tis the big night, you know, the board meeting. I have to make my appearance early."

"Sit down, sit down," said Jack, and Francis crossed to the sofa and stiffly lowered his burly figure onto the cushions. His movements had the portentousness of the clandestine drinker. He smelled strongly, too, of pastilles. "Lovely place you have," he said, dropping his guard's cap on his knee.

"I'll take that," said Jack and whisked the cap away into the bedroom.

When he returned, Francis was running a finger over the cut glass decanter on the coffee table. "My Aunt Bride had one of these in the old country."

"I got it with Green Stamps."

"Think of that," Francis said in polite astonishment. "A lovely thing like that now."

"How about a drink?" Jack asked, reaching for the ice and pouring liquid into the glasses from the decanter.

"I won't say no." He paused irresolutely. " 'Tis Jack Daniel's in the package."

"So's this. Knew you liked it. On the rocks?"

"Ah, ye know my weakness," said Francis, accepting the glass and holding it out till Jack clinked glasses. "Here's to friendship!"

"Friendship," Jack echoed and sipped his glass as Francis drank up.

"They were grand men, all three merchant seamen," Francis was declaiming. "They sailed the ports of the world but they kept their flats in New York City. 'Twas home to them, you see. Whenever they took time off, 'twas back here they came for their pleasure. Whenever they was in port, we went to the trotters or to fine dinners at places like Cavanaugh's. If the horses was running at Belmont, we went to Belmont, if Aqueduct, we went to Aqueduct. And they knew all the high-class houses. You mind what I mean by houses." He gave Jack a knowing look, his ears flaming with drink and nostalgia.

"I was the youngest, and it amused them, you see, introducing me to worldly places. Though I must say they watched over me like fathers. 'Twas like having three fathers. They were tender in their care as guardian angels."

Jack arched his eyebrows at this flight of Irish fancy, but Francis, not to be forced to earth, sailed on.

"But they was older, there's the rub, much older. Ducky and his brother was in their fifties and Calhoun was maybe closer to sixty," he said with abrupt melancholy. Holding his glass, he rested his head on the sofa back. Jack had removed the luncheon plates, and Francis raised his feet to the coffee table and crossed his ankles. A look of annoyance rippled across Jack's face but Francis had closed his eyes and didn't notice. A moment later the look was gone.

"Did they all die?" asked Jack.

Francis opened his eyes. "They did not. 'Twas a queer

thing—they took their pensions from the Seamen's Union and they all retired to Tucson, Arizona."

"Arizona!" Jack refilled Francis's glass from the decanter. The level had drastically sunk in the past two hours.

"After long years at sea they took a fancy to go live in the desert. Two years ago they pooled together and bought a house outside of Tucson. On my vacation last year I took the Greyhound bus to visit. 'Twas all barrel cactuses and white sun blazing. A wilderness!" Francis gave a great sigh. " 'Tis a blow to a man losing his friends all at once."

Jack made an affirmative noise, and after a moment Francis shot him a cagey glance.

"I'm thinking I'm too much alone with nothing to do but watch the television. Taking me meals alone with no one to talk to. 'Tis a bitter, unnatural life."

Jack lit a cigarette uneasily.

"I'm thinking to share a place with some man." He ran his gaze about Jack's living room. "Somebody with two rooms perhaps, who'd not object to cutting a high rent in half."

"My rent's all right," said Jack.

"Or who is lonely himself," Francis pressed.

Jack gave a quick nervous laugh. "I'm really some kind of hermit."

"A hermit living in New York City? And didn't I hear you was already after taking a roomer?"

Jack frowned. "Who said so?"

"The blond manicurist—that Chris. I hear the two of you talking about a roomer you had named Walter. 'Twas before the day we met before them idols in the museum."

"He wasn't a roomer. He was broke and I took him in till he got on his feet."

In the lowering silence Francis polished off his drink and glared at his shoetips.

"Maybe you're after just high-toned roomers," he

muttered mutinously. And as Jack didn't answer, he added more audibly: "Maybe I'm not high-toned enough to suit you."

His tone shocked Jack into action. Flashing a bright smile, he refilled Francis's glass from the decanter. "What's more high-toned than a man who's friends with the Governor?"

"I'm only a guard in his museum," Francis glowered. "Don't be trying to flatter me."

"A friend is who you turn to when there's trouble. When his wife was so sick and had to go to the sanatorium—"

But Francis slammed his huge palm on the coffee table. "Ye think I'm a fool greenhorn who'll lap up all yer blarney! Well, I'm not that. You can find yourself another greenhorn!"

"What's that supposed to mean?" Jack asked coldly.

Francis's heavy face was suddenly red; sweat stood out on his forehead. "It means today's your day off. You don't have to be at the bar tonight. And tonight the Governor comes to the board meeting."

"I don't follow." Jack's words fell like icicles.

"You wouldn't be trying to make me drunk? Then you could put on me uniform and fandango out of here to meet the Governor?"

"You're crazy!"

"Am I now?" Francis asked him with a look of peasant sagacity.

Slowly he raised himself to his full height. For an instant he swayed, then with mighty effort he steadied and held out his great palm like a salver. "I'll thank you for me hat," he said.

Jack seemed to verge on explosion. But under the leverage of Francis's gaze he turned and went to the bedroom. He returned with the green guard's cap.

"Now I'll go get me a pot of strong black coffee," said Francis. He placed the cap on his head, strode to the door,

and unlocked it. Jack stood listening as the heavy foot-
steps descended the marble stairs.

An hour later Jack was sitting in Steve Cameron's
headquarters at Columbus Circle.

He said, "I thought I ought to help him get to be
President."

"Great! We need all the help we can get now," the girl
said. She was pretty and pleasant and was wearing a straw
hat with a band that read: VOTE FOR CAMERON!
Her engagement ring looked like a real diamond and her
hair had the natural gloss of the rich. She glanced up from
the card that bore Jack's name and address. "Are you a
registered Democrat?"

"Well, no," Jack said. "I just lately got into this
political business."

She checked a little box. "Be sure to register so you can
vote in the New York primary."

"Does Cameron come in here a lot?" Jack asked.

"Once in a while. Of course, right now he's busy
campaigning in Illinois and Florida. Do you type?"

"What?"

"Do you use a typewriter? Could you type letters for
us?"

He looked uneasy. "My spelling's kind of shaky."

Her smile was brilliant. "So's mine. Isn't it awful? How
about calling on constituents?"

"Pardon?"

"You know, house to house, in the evenings." She
glanced at his card. "No, I forgot, you work in the
evenings." She checked another box. "Well, in the daytime
you could help man one of our stations." And as he
looked puzzled: "We have tables on busy sidewalks. You
could give out pamphlets and bumper stickers."

"What I thought was I could work right here. Maybe
take a phone or like that."

"Mm," she said. "The trouble with headquarters is

there's barely standing room. Where we need people is on the stations."

"Or I could drive for him. Or maybe be his guard. He ought to have a guard."

Surprise flickered in her blue eyes and was instantly extinguished. "Actually, the Secret Service does that. But I'll tell you what—" She handed him a stack of flyers from a great pile beside her desk. "You can pass these out at the Columbus Circle subway. Rush hour is almost ready to begin. You stand at the entrance and give them to people as they pass."

She reached into a carton box behind her and handed him a straw hat like her own. "Here, you'll need a hat." He took the hat with his free hand. "Then next time you come in, we'll assign you a station close to where you live." She looked at the card again. "Next week we'll be setting up outside the bus terminal. Okay?"

Her phone rang and she picked it up and began to talk. In a moment, seeing him still sitting beside her desk, she smiled again, her blue eyes vague, and gave him a dismissing nod.

He started to speak, then changed his mind and rose. She was still talking into the receiver as he picked his way across the red carpet under the red, white, and blue bunting. Young people, some his own age and some much younger, were manning the desks, laughing, snatching up the constantly ringing phones. The girls were all pretty with clean, moist skin and easy manners. The men looked educated in rich schools, probably Groton and Yale and like that. Jack Frost walked out the front door.

Halfway down the block, he came to a wire mesh trash basket. He dropped the stack of flyers into it.

He topped the flyers with the straw hat.

Chapter 9

On board the commercial flight from New York to Chicago, Elissa found both Dolans, Steve's campaign pollster, his media expert, his press secretary, a handful of politicians she didn't know, two socialite friends of Jim Cameron's widow, and a half dozen newsmen. As she took pictures for the politicians to show back home, she dismissed the thought of telling Steve about her vision. She would have less chance to talk on the plane than she did in New York. And since she'd seen his death in the museum, he should be safe until they got back to New York.

At O'Hare the Illinois advance man rushed up the ramp with the latest schedule—a whirlwind trip to Rockford, Peoria, Springfield, Decatur, and Urbana. From then on she only registered disconnected fragments: the terminal crowds carrying signs WIN WITH STEVE and sporting campaign hats and buttons; the Boeing 727 charter jets that took them on their swing around the state.

She had a blurred sense of landings, motorcades, crowds, blitzing shopping centers with leaflets. Steve making speeches at Lions Clubs, American Legion posts, labor halls, factory shift lines. She took pictures at press conferences and cocktail party fund raisers, driving endlessly to the next town where she fell asleep after midnight in a strange motel room. But she was up by six the next morning to take her pictures to a quick print shop, to cover Steve's interview at the local newspaper, the Shriners' Hospital for crippled children, in time for lunch at a shopping mall.

Once, at one of the shopping centers, the blur focused. Steve was finishing his speech when the crowd seemed to coalesce, become a single creature. As it roared toward him, Elissa had a rushing sense of danger. She tried to see which way the aides clearing a path for Steve were moving. Then a woman screamed and she stood frozen. An aide scooped up a fallen child and Steve held it a moment, then returned it to its mother. He made his way to the open convertible, climbed into it, waved, smiling imperturbably, and the motorcade pulled out for City Hall. Her sense of danger faded.

On the third evening she passed Steve's room as she went toward the motel coffee shop for dinner. His door was open and he was sitting on his bed in shirt sleeves, phoning. When he saw her, he signaled her to come inside. For a moment she was afraid he wanted the day's pictures before they went on for his television appearance. But she went in and stood by his bedside.

"Hold on," he said into the phone, and asked her, "Where were you going?"

"Dinner. If we leave for the talk show by seven thirty—"

He held up his hand and went back to the phone. "Double the order," he said and replaced the instrument. "Have dinner here. Steak, fries, tomatoes. I want to talk to you."

He got up, fetched two glasses from the bathroom, dropped in ice from the ice bucket, and added vodka. "Can you drink it on the rocks?" He handed her a glass, walked to the door, and closed it. "I don't like the way you look," he said.

It seemed almost like an accusation. She regarded him in dismay.

"I know we're working you too hard. You're not getting enough sleep or eating properly. Five cities in three days —but that's campaigning. And it won't get any better."

He paused but she didn't know where he was headed, so she was silent.

"It's only March. We go on till the California primary. If we win, there's the nominating convention. After that, the campaign gets hotter." He hesitated. "I don't think you can handle it, Elissa."

So that was it. She could hardly believe in such injustice. "Why did you ask me on the trip if you were going to fire me?"

His blue eyes darkened. Distress shadowed the hawklike face. "Now you wait," he said. He took her drink, set it alongside his on the nightstand, caught her hand, and drew her down to sit beside him. "How can you talk about firing? I just don't like what this campaign is doing to you. Listen, Elissa I've known you since you were—what?— twelve?"

"Thirteen."

"And you were the strangest, loveliest child I ever met. Do you know what I do when things go wrong for me? I shut off my mind and go back to those days on Tarpon Island. I picture the sea, bumming around in the boat, the reefs. Not diving for anything, just seeing. Do you know what I'm trying to say?"

"I'm not sure."

"Do you remember the day we ran down to Boca Grande?"

She nodded. "In your Mako. I'd always wanted to go but it was too far for the skiff."

"What else happened?"

She drew her pale brows together, recapturing the day.

"It was glassed off. We dived the rocks off Woman Key and saw a school of tarpon. Then we ran along to Boca Grande. We ... anchored?"

"What else?"

"Went ashore. Maybe explored a little. Coming back we dived the wreck—"

"Before that. The conch," he prompted.

She looked at him blankly.

"You found a shell on the beach. A queen conch, in perfect condition. When we were leaving, I thought you'd forgotten it. But when I asked if you wanted to take it, you said it belonged there. I've never forgotten."

She smiled unsurely. "I don't like to bring them home."

"The Camerons do, I'm afraid. We have to bring it all home. We snatch and grab. We fight to win. We're predators. You're not a predator, Elissa."

"I'm strong and healthy. I'll become one."

He laughed. "God forbid! I feel guilty already for dragging you into the campaign rat race."

"Why don't you stop?" And at his surprise: "If it's a rat race, why don't you quit, get out?"

He gazed at her as if he were trying to tell if she was serious. "You really mean it," he said at last. "You'd do it in my place."

"Maybe not," she said, struck by his expression. It was as if he were watching a creature utterly alien. And how did she dare question a Cameron, a Governor, perhaps a President? "Maybe I wouldn't. I guess your father would be disappointed."

He grinned. "I'll bet he would. No, Elissa, I'll run my race. But I don't like what it's doing to you."

"It's not the work," she said, getting up her courage. "I mean, it's not the hours or anything. It's hard to explain, but the night in the museum—"

"I was wrong," he said quickly. "I'm sorry. I didn't expect it to happen."

"That's all right," she said, though desolation struck her. "It didn't mean anything."

"No, it didn't. Compared to what we had already." He took both her hands so she had to look at him. "Dammit, Elissa, you're my *child*. You're not just a girl, a woman. You're part of a private place I can escape to."

"I don't want to be your child," she objected.

"Not a child then. Something stranger—a mermaid maybe?"

His smile enticed her from some place of danger. Not understanding, she let herself be enticed, smiled back tentatively, and relieved, he leaned to kiss her forehead, slowly touched her nose with his lips, pressed her mouth lightly. "You're more than that."

"Hey, Steve, we've fucked up in Urbana! There's a student rally—" Jay Dolan had rapped briefly and thrown the door open. He stopped in the doorway, his hands full of papers. "Whoops, sorry." His eager look clouded. The dark eyes grew almost black with annoyance.

"Come on in," Steve said resignedly. "Where's the rally?"

"University of Illinois here in Urbana. Tonight. They figure there'll be at least two thousand students. Cy should have booked you in." Cy was the Illinois advance man. Jay had already recovered from his surprise and was driving ahead as if he hadn't intruded. The only sign he gave was ignoring Elissa. "Shall we try to work you in? It could be just a drop-in visit."

"I've got the talk show."

"That's at eight. You could hit the campus by nine thirty."

As the waiter arrived with their dinner order, Elissa rose from the bed and strolled to the window.

"Jane called from Miami," Jay said. "Her photographer's either on drugs or he's a sex maniac. She says he's all over her like a pet squirrel."

"Oh God." Jim's widow, Jane, was campaigning in

Florida and despite her background as an actress was the most straitlaced of the Camerons. "Better let him go."

"She already did that herself. Thing is, she's got a heavy schedule tomorrow—the Miami *Herald*, a TV show, a hospital. I'll spare you the rest. She needs another photographer."

"Give her one."

"He's with your mother in Tallahassee."

"We only have two photographers in Florida?"

"Four. Two are down with the flu." He paused. "How about sending Elissa? If she goes out tonight, she'd be in time to cover Jane in Miami. The student rally will have the campus news photographer. And you're leaving yourself for Florida tomorrow."

"When does she sleep?"

"On the plane. Like we all do."

Steve sighed. "Well, Elissa?"

She turned from the window. She knew he was asking, really, if she'd drop out of the whole campaign. She could return to The New School. She could go back to the keys. Or she could hang on for the entire ride. It would be harder to hang on, though, with Jay alerted. She read real dislike in his gaze now, a naked warning. Too, she dimly understood that she was endangering what Steve valued of their past. He'd told her so when he'd said she couldn't handle campaigning.

And yet, not to see him for months, years even, without the chance to warn him of the future— She could not do it. She knew he would ignore the warnings.

She would stay.

As soon as the talk show was over, a staff car took her to the airport and she spent most of the night making her way to Miami—the charter jet to Chicago, waiting at O'Hare to continue by commercial airline, then the endless ride over freeways till she fell into a hotel bed in Miami Beach.

She was no sooner asleep than her phone rang. She groped on her nightstand while she dazedly regarded palm fronds beyond the balcony. She was home. No, she wasn't. You couldn't see palm trees from her bunk on the houseboat. Besides, Sam and Delia had moved the houseboat to the yacht club. But the air was warm and soft with moisture, and she smelled jasmine and the ocean. It was Miami and Jane Cameron was scheduled to meet the Miami *Herald* staff at nine. Her fingers finally found the phone.

She moved rapidly through the day with Jane and two young men from the Miami headquarters. After the meeting in the *Herald* building, they visited three coffee hours set up by local women, then on to a children's hospital. Lunch in a shopping mall was a blitz of leaflets, Cameron buttons, and bumper stickers. Then an old-age home in Miami Beach, on to a Mother House for retired nuns, a television show, and back to the hotel to catch a hamburger while she showered and dressed. That evening Jane spoke before eight hundred women at an American Legion post and they went to another rally after. It was nearly midnight when Elissa got back to her room.

But all day, as she had photographed Jane and local Democrats, she had been thinking of the Dolans. As clearly as if he had been before her, she pictured Jay, dark, intense, his eyes clouding with anger when he saw Steve kissing her. Was it she herself he disliked? Or was it Steve's distraction from the campaign that he resented? She had always sensed the force of his ambition. Perhaps he thought she was too young, that nineteen was flighty, that Steve needed someone steadier and older. Or maybe he feared Sam Blake's obstreperous reputation and thought she'd turn out like her father. After all, he had seen Steve through the trouble with Cathy. He might view her as a second Cathy and feel Steve couldn't weather another such disaster.

His own choice for a politician's wife had been Amanda: pretty, witty, well-born, an easy, experienced campaigner.

While she was . . . what? An untried girl raised by a drunken radical on a houseboat in the Florida keys. The thought of hostessing a Governor's dinner dismayed her. And the White House would be even more dreadful. Whatever she was, she was certainly nothing like Amanda.

Undressing, she suddenly wondered if Jay was himself pushing Amanda at Steve to hold him safe in their own circle. It seemed impossibly perverse for a husband to do that, and yet he constantly brought Amanda along where Steve was campaigning. She often traveled with Steve in his charter jet when Jay wasn't present. Amanda had, in fact, become Steve's unofficial hostess. If Jay knew of the gossip, he was at no pains to change the conditions that caused it. Perhaps to keep Steve undistracted, Jay would really do anything.

On the other hand, Steve should not be led so easily. As she buttoned her pajama top, she was suddenly angry at Steve for letting Jay manipulate him. The way he had, for instance, when Steve had agreed to her leaving Urbana.

Surprised, she sat on the bed and considered her own anger. First she had been jealous and now she was angry. Angry at *Steve*. A month ago she would have thought that he couldn't make her angry. Drawing up her legs tailor fashion, she had an awed sense of herself turning into something strangely different. The thought struck her: Maybe *I* might kill him. Perhaps that was what she had seen in the museum—she would be so jealous and angry that she herself would pick up the gun.

Chilled, she went on staring at the palms outside her window until, to shake off the thought, she reached across the bed for the phone.

She gave Sam Blake's number to the hotel operator and after four rings it was answered. But this time it wasn't Sam. She recognized the soft rushing voice so unlikely in a middle-aged schoolteacher.

"Hi, Delia," she said, forcing back panic and trying for a cheerful note. "Hope I didn't wake you."

"We're up—it's okay. But it's after eleven—is something wrong? Has anything happened?"

"I'm fine," she lied as her heart sank. Delia was so easily alarmed that she could never bring herself to upset her. "I'm in Miami."

"Miami!" cried Delia.

"Campaigning for Cameron," Elissa said with deliberate calm. "The Florida primary's coming up. It's just routine."

"When will you be down? I'll start getting your room ready!"

"No!" she almost shouted. She pictured the whirlwind of Sam's being turned out of his office and wished Delia would stop trying to be a loving stepmother. "We're so busy I can't get away. I just called to say hello." She paused. "Is Sam around?"

"I'll call him," said Delia, too quickly, and in a few minutes Sam came to the phone.

"Hi, dad, it's me. Were you busy?"

"Just washing the new dog. We're going to call her Lady. Picked her up at the pound a couple of minutes before the executioner."

"That's great," she said hollowly. Not that she wasn't glad for the dog. But Sam's life seemed to have closed over the gap of her absence; it was hard to find an opening.

"What's this I hear about your being in Miami?"

"I'm on the windup for the Florida primary taking pictures of Jane Cameron. I'm afraid I'm going to be too busy—"

"You really like politics?" he asked in wonder. "It always bored me."

"Well," she began, and to her consternation, found herself fighting tears. While she fought them, she was silent.

And as if he sensed some of her trouble in the silence, he asked, "Sure you don't want to come home, toots?"

But, of course, she couldn't come home, not since she'd had the vision of Steve's murder. Not so long as there was a chance to stop its happening. "Was mother psychic?" she suddenly asked him.

"Was she *what?*"

She remembered too late his disbelief in anything that couldn't be seen, heard, touched, or measured. "Cloud-cuckoo-land" was his term for astrology, palmistry, psychic phenomena, and every known religion. "I ran into a woman named Valdez," she said, trying to head off "cloud-cuckoo-land." "She knew the Verricks in the Village. She said my mother saw the future."

"The dyke painter?" he laughed. "Don't listen to Valdez. She used to help Elinor bring in her messages from Lord Byron on the Ouija board."

"But Mother foretold the death of Valdez's father. And then my grandfather—she saw his head all bloody—"

"Old Valdez," he chuckled. "Imagine your meeting Valdez. She must be well past seventy." He made it sound as if Valdez was senile.

"But if it wasn't drugs that made mother psychotic! If she was psychic and we sent her to Chattahoochee—"

"Whoa there!"

"—A lot of people in institutions are really psychic!"

A sudden silence.

Finally Sam said, "Are you okay, hon? That political crowd is damned fast company."

She wanted to scream, "Those insects she saw were Elinor's brain cancer!" But she knew how it would sound to Sam, so she didn't.

"Why not drop out for a few weeks?" Sam asked with false casualness. "Come visit. Go out in the boat, swim, dive, relax."

She took a breath to make her voice steady. "Maybe later. After California."

"I think you ought to lay back awhile."

"I'm okay, dad. It was just meeting Valdez."

"Oh, Valdez," he said, relieved to be able to dismiss notions brought on by Valdez.

"I'll see you next time I'm down. I promise," she said miserably. "I love you."

"Love you too, toots," he said and hung up.

As she put the phone into its cradle, she told herself she'd been too blunt about Valdez. She knew his psi prejudice and she shouldn't have attacked it so directly. Of course, he would scoff at an old woman's claims that Veronica had foretold a man's death in Texas, the bloody head of her own grandfather. How could he be expected to value a witness like Valdez who took down spirit messages?

Even if Sam himself had witnessed Veronica's prophecies, he wouldn't have admitted them. Not out of dishonesty, but because they wouldn't fit the real world as he saw it. He simply wouldn't have been able to accept those kinds of facts. Just as he hadn't matched up Veronica's evil insects with Elinor's brain being invaded by brain cancer. She herself hadn't seen a connection until Don had underlined it.

Sitting on the hotel bed, she probed her memory for more visions like the evil insects, other times they had thought Veronica was on drugs or crazy when she may have been looking into the future and been terrified by the awful events rushing down upon her. Perhaps even in Big Sur, beating her hands against the windowpane, Veronica had not seen a windowpane but Chattahoochee and Manhattan State, the years of wire mesh and strait-jackets.

Then her thoughts abruptly switched direction and she wondered if Don Young was also fitting events to his own world picture. He wanted psi to exist, so he saw a pattern emerging. Maybe, she thought, people create their world by what they believe in. For an instant she felt she verged on understanding something of vital importance.

But she was too tired to maintain the clear focus. The idea blurred and she fell back into the painful round of her earlier thinking.

If Don, too, was trying to fit events to theory, he might be wrong about the inmates of insane asylums having psi talent. Perhaps Veronica's evil insects were a common symptom of psychosis and Elinor's brain cancer might be just coincidence. And if he were wrong about Veronica, he might also be wrong about Elissa. Perhaps her visions were, after all, hallucinations—seeing Steve's death, hearing voices in the elevator, even the torch-bearing mob in nineteenth-century costume—simply signs of her own mind's disintegration.

In an effort to stop the millrace of her thoughts, she took a hot shower, put on her pajama top again, brushed her hair, drank a glass of water, and turned down the bed. Sternly, she even turned off the lights and crept between the covers. But she couldn't sleep.

Exasperated with herself, she jumped up and went across to the chair where she'd hung her shoulder bag. Rummaging through it, she found the little bronze water spirit that Steve had given her on her birthday. Last night he'd mentioned mermaids and it seemed more than ever to link them. Holding it tightly, she went back to bed and, still clutching the little water spirit, slept.

Later she was unable to recollect her dream clearly. She remembered drifting by mangroves in her skiff. Then somehow she had fallen out of the boat. She'd lost her flippers and was swimming against a racing current. A buoy appeared marked 62. She was trying to reach it but a choppy sea kept washing over her and she knew she couldn't make it. She tried to scream but water poured in her mouth—

"Elissa!"

It was Steve. Really Steve before her, holding her tightly by her shoulders. "What are you doing out here?"

She gazed about her, dazed. She was on a balcony.

Then, seeing the palms and poincianas, she remembered. She had come to Miami to photograph Jane Cameron. She was in Miami Beach. But what was she doing on a balcony? She looked down. She was just wearing her pajama top. Why wasn't she in bed?

"It's okay," Steve said to the men standing behind him. They were in ties and business suits. Secret Service men.

"She's been working too hard," Steve said. "I guess it got to her."

"Want us to get her to her room, Governor?"

"I'll do it."

"Need help?"

"It won't be necessary."

"Good night to you then," the man said reluctantly. "We'll be right here if you need us." He turned and entered a room that faced on the balcony, his partner following.

"All right, Elissa," Steve said, "which one's yours?"

She looked at the long balcony that ran along the Cameron staff rooms. "I'm not sure. Wait, maybe that one with the palm tree. What happened?"

"Do you have a bottle in your room?"

"No." Did he think she'd been drinking?

"In here then." He walked her through two open French doors into a strange hotel bedroom. It must be his suite. Through the door she could see a sitting room.

He opened a leather suitcase, took out a vodka bottle, poured liquid into two glasses on the bureau, and dropped in ice cubes from a bucket. "Do you often sleepwalk?"

"Never! Well, maybe as a child, I guess I did. But not for years. Was that what it was? Sleepwalking?"

"I'm afraid so. Cathy was . . . somnambulistic. Sometimes." She guessed from his hesitation that it had been when she was drinking.

"But I hadn't had anything! I'd been covering Jane all day. After dinner she talked at the Legion and a rally. I came back here and went to sleep and had a nightmare."

She stopped, her lips still parted, as the dream-terror reached out for her again.

"Drink that," he said, and as she obediently sipped her drink, he raised his glass to her, sat back on the bed, and crossed his ankles. "Tell me about it."

"I can't remember too well," she said slowly. "I was in the skiff near some mangroves. Then I must have fallen out of the boat because I was swimming somewhere else. Out at sea, or maybe a ship's channel. There was a buoy marked sixty-two. I was trying to reach it but I couldn't. There was a current and I'd lost my flippers. The chop was washing me back but I was trying—I kept seeing the number sixty-two."

"Hope it's our score in the Florida primary."

She was silent.

"Sorry, hon. I'm not really taking it lightly. I know you're upset. But it was only a dream. What I don't like is the sleepwalking. Those Secret Service men could have jumped you. You could have fallen. Or walked off the balcony." He finished his drink, went back to the bureau, and indicated the bottle. She shook her head.

"How about going home while you're in Miami?" he asked. But at the look on her face, he tried to soften it. "For just a day or two. Get some sun, take it easy, go diving—"

"No. Please, Steve."

He nodded with reluctance. "But if it happens again, you're on the bench. No argument."

Before he could change his mind, she drank off her vodka, went into the bathroom, and threw the ice cubes into the basin. A self-effacing impulse made her rinse out the glass and replace it where it had been before she'd troubled his arrival.

When she returned to the bedroom, she saw that he had carried his fresh drink back to the bed. She paused in the doorway. He had drawn the drapes to shut out the view of the balcony and turned off his nightstand light.

It might be, after all, the night she'd hoped for, the time they'd have no interruptions. She'd made up her mind to see a doctor for the pill, but before she could do it, he had rushed her off to Chicago. Yet, how could she not do what she most wanted—

All of a sudden her mind stopped.

Lit only by the shaft of light from the bathroom, it looked like the shadowed bedroom in the museum.

"What's wrong, Elissa?" he asked in concern, and she realized she was still frozen in the doorway. He set his drink on the nightstand, rose from the bed, and put his arms around her. "What's the matter?"

In that moment she wanted to cry, to confide in him, and tell him about her vision of his death. But she remembered his flippancy about her dream of drowning and she hesitated.

"Come here," he said, drawing her down on the bed beside him. He took her head between his hands and looked into her face. "Poor love, I'm not taking much care of you, am I? First we work you half to death and then we fly you around when you should be sleeping. And when you sleepwalk, the Secret Service jumps you. No wonder you're upset."

Not trusting her voice, she shook her head to tell him he was wrong, but he brushed her cheeks with his thumbs and she realized with surprise that tears were slipping down her face.

"Don't cry, love," he said gently. Bending toward her, he kissed her forehead, and when she smiled, he drew her into his arms and held her. "Do you want to stay here tonight?" he asked.

As she nodded against his chest, he raised her face again and pressed his mouth to hers. Suddenly, urgency overcame her, a need to shelter against him from her new, frightening knowledge.

"Sweet Elissa," he murmured.

She knew then that she wasn't going to tell him what

she'd seen in the museum. Because she couldn't be sure anymore that it would happen in the museum.

All darkened bedrooms looked alike.

And she no longer knew where his death would take place.

On primary night Sam and Delia were standing by the rear entrance to the hotel ballroom when Steve came downstairs for his television appearance.

Carter had actually taken the state. But Carter had campaigned hard in Florida, while Steve, concentrating on Massachusetts, Wisconsin, and New York, hadn't. So Steve's good showing was actually a victory.

The volunteers packed into the ballroom were exuberant and Old Tom, Mary, and Jane Cameron were glowing as they swept after Steve into the ballroom. Jay and Amanda were with them, as well as Elissa, who had been shooting family pictures in Steve's suite—Old Tom democratically eating a hamburger, Steve in shirt sleeves watching the three TV sets. She was flushed from the evening, so that she was almost past Sam before she saw him. Then she shouted and threw her arms about him.

"Daddy!" she shouted.

He grinned, held out his arms, and she flew into them and kissed him.

"Surprised?" he asked with complacence.

"But how? What made you come to a primary night? I'm dumbfounded."

"Steve called us and arranged for passes. Not that the SS didn't frisk us before we got into the ballroom." He seemed quite pleased by the frisking. Looking at his bony, ruined features, Elissa guessed he was enjoying a nostalgic trip: Sam Blake, dangerous radical of the 1960s.

She squeezed his hand and turned to Delia, who was standing to one side, her smile strained from the strength of wanting to be included.

"Delia." As Elissa kissed her cheek, Delia's lips trembled

as if she might cry. But then the television lights blazed for Steve's appearance. Slowly, while he was talking, Delia seemed to grow calmer.

His stint before the cameras over, Steve returned to them. And under the impact of the Cameron charisma, Elissa was happy to see that Delia brightened and began unconsciously smoothing down her sweater. Then Steve said to Sam, "We're working Elissa too hard. She needs time off before we go back."

Elissa glanced at him and was relieved that he was smiling.

"I'm fine, daddy."

"She looks okay to me," Sam said. "How's she doing?"

"Better than my pollsters. She forecast sixty-two delegates for Florida," Steve grinned. "Of course her methods are unorthodox—"

Sam caught the teasing note, half smiled, then shot her a look.

"I dreamed it," she told him imploringly.

The smile stayed on his face but his eyes grew troubled and she guessed he was remembering that she'd asked him if Veronica was psychic.

"It was only a dumb dream, daddy," she told him more urgently.

He nodded and she tried to think of what else she could say to relieve his concern.

It was at that moment that she saw Jack Frost.

She saw him clearly—the angular face beneath the thinning hair, caught even a look of recognition in the blue eyes beneath the scar that puckered his right eyebrow. He was wearing a modish safari jacket.

"Steve," she said, but he was talking to Jay. When she looked back, Jack Frost had vanished. She scanned the crowd that was packing the ballroom: the volunteers, their guests, the fans, the freaks, the pressmen, TV electricians. He was nowhere.

She began to think she had just imagined him. Mist

seemed to be graying the area between present reality and dreams, between her visions of the past and the future. She glanced toward Sam and caught him gazing at her, his fine-boned face disturbed. He was, she knew, remembering the years with Veronica. Hoping it wasn't starting over again.

Chapter 10

"We know a few things about precognition, Elissa," Don Young said above his plate of spaghetti at Jenny's dinner table. "For example, it's apt to be triggered by stress."

Steve had refused to take her on his swing of Wisconsin; he'd been too concerned about her sleepwalking. But when she had balked at returning to Key West, they had compromised on New York headquarters. At least, she felt, that kept her in touch. He had also given orders about her work load, and they had cut out her night assignments. Since she was free, she had come to Jenny's for dinner.

"You mean like in a war or a plane accident?" asked Elissa.

"Not just physical stress." He poured more Chianti into his wineglass. "Let's take your first vision. Seeing Cameron's death. You'd just been making love—"

Elissa looked startled and Jenny protested, "Don!"

"This is for science," said Don.

"And the nearer you get to the coming event, the better the reception," said Al hurriedly. "We checked the New

York Premonitions Registry and nothing has come in yet on a Cameron assassination. So we probably have some time left."

"There's a registry for premonitions?"

"Four registries—in London, New York, Monterey, and Toronto," said Don. "Robert Nelson runs ours from Maimonides Hospital. It's modeled after the London Premonitions Bureau, which was started by a British psychiatrist and the science editor of the *Evening Standard*."

"But what do they do?" Elissa asked.

"People send in their precognitive dreams and premonitions. So if they happen, they've been recorded beforehand. That way nobody can say it was knowledge after the fact. Eventually they'll act as an early warning system to prevent disaster."

"Can you prevent it?" asked Elissa. "That boy from the psi lab said—"

"Oh Billy! She met Billy the night she slid back to the draft riots," explained Don to Al. "Somebody must have told him about Louisa Rhine's study."

"Who's Louisa Rhine?" asked Elissa.

"Louisa Rhine," Don said in the tone of a man who's been asked who was Albert Einstein, "is a lovely, white-haired lady who's the widow of Dr. J. B. Rhine, the card-guessing man. Dr. Louisa worked with him. Her *Hidden Channels of the Mind* was a milestone in parapsychology. She has collected fourteen thousand cases of spontaneous premonitions and probably knows more than anyone else about prophetic warnings."

"But didn't she say you couldn't avert them?"

"Not quite. The score is they were averted nine times out of a hundred and ninety," said Al. "Which isn't much, but it shows it can be done."

"Give her the baby's crib case," said Don.

"Okay. A mother dreamed that in two hours a storm would loosen a chandelier, which would fall into her baby's crib and kill it. She woke. It was calm weather but she went to the crib and got her baby. Two hours later, just as she'd dreamed, a storm blew down the chandelier. It crashed where the baby's head would have been."

Don said, "So if we had more details on Cameron's death, we could remove the baby."

"Why not remove the crib?" asked Jenny. "Elissa saw it happening in the museum. So keep him out of the museum."

"I'm not sure it was in the museum," confessed Elissa. "His hotel room in Miami Beach looked the same. It was dark, just a light coming from the bathroom."

"Let's try *time* then," said Jenny. "Maybe you saw something we could use as a clue. A calendar maybe, or a newspaper. Even flowers might pinpoint the season."

"Anemones!" said Elissa. "There were anemones."

"There you are. Anemones are spring flowers. It's to happen before spring is over."

"Or next spring," Don said. "But that's doubtful. Too far ahead for such a clear precognition."

"Besides, they were in the sitting room," said Elissa. "I might have quit seeing the future by the time I got there. I'm pretty sure I saw them when we first went in."

"So much for when and where," said Don. "That leaves who. Sure you can't tell us more about the assassin?"

"All I heard was men shouting. I couldn't even hear what they—" She stopped.

Don jumped on it. "What did you think of?"

She was silent, thinking quickly. If they were both men, then the assassin couldn't be a woman, so she could dismiss the fear that she herself might kill him. The relief was enormous. But she couldn't bring herself to confess that she was jealous of Amanda. "Nothing," she said. "I was trying to remember what they said but it was too blurry."

"If we could only bring back a broader angle of memory." Don polished off his Chianti with decision. "We'll have to try hypnosis."

Elissa frowned, not liking the idea of giving control of her mind to another person. She'd refused once before but here he was again, proposing it.

"You can see your conscious memory isn't enough, Elissa. The only ways left to open your mind and pinpoint the time are drugs and hypnosis. If you want to try and avert Cameron's murder . . ." Don left his sentence trailing.

She sighed. "Okay."

"Which one do you pick?"

"Hypnosis."

He put a finger in his pocket and fished out a gold pen.

"You are in a deep trance, Elissa. It's a pleasant and safe feeling. You are relaxed completely. You feel wonderful all over," Don was saying. His tone was gentle and persuasive.

Elissa sat in the wing chair in the darkened living room of Jenny's apartment, her eyes closed, her pale hair veiling her face as she slumped forward.

Don glanced at Al and Jenny, then pocketed the gold pen that she'd stared at while she was being hypnotized. "Let's test," he told them.

"Your left arm is heavy," he continued softly. "Imagine a lead weight is dragging your wrist down." Slowly, Elissa leaned to the left until her left hand rested on the braided rug. "I'm releasing your wrist from the lead weight."

Her arm returned to her lap.

"Elissa," he said, "you're going to go back to the night of your birthday. You will be in the museum in Cameron's suite. You will see and hear everything distinctly. When I count to three, you'll find yourself back taking a shower in the bathroom. You'll describe everything you hear and see just as it's happening. Okay, here we go— one, two, three."

Slowly, Elissa rose from the wing chair, adjusted an invisible shower mechanism, and threw back her head to enjoy the play of water. She took an invisible cake of soap from a recess, sniffed it, put it back, and turned to let the water stream over her neck and shoulders. She turned again and let it strike her breastbone. At last she reached to turn off the tap, then froze, listening.

"Tell us what you hear and see," Don commanded softly.

"Voices," she said. "Men shouting. They're angry. Steve—I think it's Steve—is yelling, 'Get the hell out!' The other man is shouting back. I can't make out the actual words, though, just a lot of yelling. 'For God's sake, don't!' Is it Steve? I don't know if it's Steve. He's alone. He was sleeping. Nobody knows about this place but the family. Who could be with him?"

Suddenly her body jerked. "A shot," she said in agitation. "Another shot." Her face contorted in distress and she stood huddled, listening. "Steve?" she whispered.

She crept forward, reached for an invisible towel, and wrapped it around her. "Steve?" she called more loudly. She pressed her ear to an invisible door, then slowly cracked it. She peered through.

"Tell us what you're seeing, Elissa," Don reminded. "And hearing, smelling, touching."

"Darkness. A mirror. A bureau. I hear a clock whirring. I smell aftershave like spice and vodka. I see a big bed. There's nobody there, I mean, nobody but Steve. He's still on the bed, he's sleeping." She pulled the invisible door toward her and peered more closely. Then she gasped. Her face noticeably paled. "Blood! Blood everywhere. All over the bed. And his head—" She drew her breath in, shuddered, struck speechless. Then a heartbroken cry escaped her.

"Stop it, Don!" Jenny cried. "Bring her out of it! This is cruel! It's dangerous! She'll crack!"

"All right, Elissa. It's just a bad dream and we're going to wake you," Don said gently. "You'll come up slowly. When I count to three, you'll feel comfortable and fully alert. You'll be pleased with yourself for doing so well in hypnosis."

"Hurry! Get her out of it," said Jenny.

"You'll open your eyes and feel good all over. Okay, Elissa, let's do it—one, two, three!"

For a moment they watched anxiously as she stood in the center of the living room, one hand held from her in horror. Then slowly the hand dropped to her side and the lovely face smoothed. She opened her eyes and looked about her, smiling.

"How did I do?"

Relieved, Don dropped into the wing chair. "You did fine. Couldn't have done better. We were there. We went through it with you."

"Did you get anything? Something I hadn't remembered?"

He raised his hands and dropped them in a futile gesture.

"Then it failed. I don't want to take drugs either."

"There's one more method we might try in order to get a wider picture. We can't get it from the scene that she *remembers*. But if she could see the future again from a different angle—"

"By suspending her in theta?" asked Jenny. She sounded disapproving.

"If we could just get a look at the assassin—"

"It's dangerous, Don! Look how she reacted!"

Elissa considered. On the one hand, Jenny said outright that it was dangerous. And even Don, now that he knew her mother's history, had been slow to suggest it. But they had no other way left to find out when Steve was going to be killed or who would be his murderer. If she didn't take the chance, Steve would continue toward his inexorably fatal future. Holding in her fear, she said, "I'm okay. I'll do it."

"Good girl," said Don. "Tomorrow's Saturday. Let's make it at two."

"Everybody has a different way of beginning," said Don. "Some people lie down, some sit up. Some take deep breaths. Billy likes a cup of coffee. You can pick your own method."

Elissa said, "I'd rather sit."

They were in the basement wing of the psychology department, in an acoustically shielded room with a camp bed, a small table, a chair, and a loudspeaker. Don was standing beside Elissa, who was in the chair with wire leads attached to her scalp.

"Now, what we're trying to do is give you another shot at what's going to happen in that museum. Only maybe with a different perspective, which might give us more clues to go on. Like time. If we're lucky, you'll get a look at the assassin. Since most psi experience happens when the brain is emitting slow brain waves, we're going to guide you down into theta waves, which are the slowest you'll have while you're conscious. If you went down farther, into delta, you'd be asleep. We don't want that. In order to prevent it, I'm going to stop you if you drop below theta."

"How will you know where I am?"

"You're hitched up to an EEG, an electroencephalograph machine. That's those wire leads on your head. They run to a brain wave machine in a room down the hall where I'll be getting a computer printout. So I'll know what kind of waves you're making. Is that clear?"

"I think so."

"The first thing you'll do is relax. Close your eyes and picture a beach till you slow your brain waves. When you're making alpha, I'll press a buzzer once. I'll press it twice if you go into theta. If you start to drift any

farther into sleep, I'll ring a bell on the loudspeaker.
You'll try to keep holed up in theta. Got it?"

Elissa nodded.

"If you get a clear picture, describe it into this
machine." He touched a tape recorder on the little table.
"If you do reach the future, we'll have it on tape,
witnessed before it happens. Now we hope you get
directly onto Cameron. But in case you don't, and yet
you're still getting *some* future, I'm setting up an alternate
target."

"What's that?"

"A strip of film I'm going to show you. I won't know
the subject myself until we pick it out at random *later*
from a pile of possible subjects. It's like the White Queen
in *Alice*. She screamed first, then got stuck with the pin."

"It sounds impossible," she said.

"It *is*," he said, pleased. "That's what makes it so
exciting. We call it double-blind conditions. Okay, we're
ready. I'll be monitoring. Don't think of it as a test. It's
just a game we're playing." He pressed a button on the
recorder. He went to the door and just before he left,
he turned and said, "You're on!"

"People skating. A girl in red leotards. Everybody's
ice-skating. Round and round. It's very pretty."

She was sitting with her eyes closed, feeling very
sleepy. So sleepy, in fact, that the warning bell had rung
twice to tell her to go back to theta. With great effort
she said: "A golden man . . . and books . . . a bowl
of flowers. . . . I see a beautiful kind of temple. But
there's a funny feeling like something bad's about to
happen. . . . I see a man's leg. There isn't any body.
The pools are all filled with blood." She was so sleepy,
she couldn't continue.

From a far distance a bell was sounding. She forced
herself to rise from the enveloping drowsiness and made

herself murmur: "A bare room like in a hospital . . . a corridor. People are running. They're helping somebody on the floor. . . . Did he fall? . . . He's jumping around like he's holding a hot wire. How could he be electrocuted on the floor?" But she was too drowsy again. The bell was ringing and she dove deeper, trying to escape. She was sheltering beneath a clump of staghorn coral. A little blue hamlet and a school of black-and-yellow sergeant majors were swimming about her. A moray peered out from a hole in the reef. She had a sense of great impending danger—

"Okay, hon. An hour's long enough the first time."

It was Don. He was beside her in the shadowed room, taking off her electrodes, washing off the paste with something sharply cold.

"How did it work?" she asked.

"Nothing on Cameron. But you may still have seen some other future." He fiddled with the recorder, punched a button, and picked out a reel of tape. "Have some coffee while we check it out."

They went down the hall to the psi lab waiting room. It had bare floors, a scruffy-looking sofa, and a rubber plant. There were three leather armchairs and a pile of magazines on a coffee table. An electric coffee maker sat on a long table beneath the pigeonhole department mailboxes, with a plastic can of sugar and a can of powdered milk, instant tea, Sanka, coffee, and a stack of paper cups beside it. Don filled a paper cup with coffee, handed it to her, and led her through a door posted with an office hours schedule into a cubicle in a state of extraordinary chaos. Professional magazines and typed papers littered the gray metal desk. Two straight-backed chairs sat against one wall. A metal book case was filled in a slipshod manner with textbooks and a projection machine was balanced on its top.

While Elissa strolled to the window, he pulled open a desk drawer and began fishing out manila envelopes.

"Oh hello, Billy," he said. "What are you doing here?"
"Just stopped by."

Elissa turned to the thin youth with the shaved skull whom she'd met the night she'd seen the draft riots. He was standing in Don's office doorway wearing an old overcoat that was too big for him and carrying a carton of sandwiches and coffee.

"I had a delivery on the next block, so I thought I'd look in."

"Glad you did. We can use you," said Don. "You can witness that I'm pulling out this envelope at random."

"You can say that again," Billy grinned as an avalanche of magazines and papers slid into the drawer from the desktop. He set down the cardboard box and took off his overcoat, revealing a Mickey Mouse shirt and a threadbare pair of corduroys. No wonder the coffee they ordered at headquarters was always cold, Elissa thought, if that's the way all messengers run lunches.

"So you're hitting the big time," Billy said. There was a puzzling truculence in his manner. Of course, she thought, he was a telepath! Don had taken him out of Rockland State Hospital and she was threatening to overshadow the only small fame he had ever known.

"I don't know if I hit anything," she said. "We haven't run the film yet."

"We'll do it now. Pull the drapes, Elissa. Close the door, Billy," said Don. He flicked a light switch and put the reel on the projector.

In another moment they were watching the winter Olympics. A commentator's voice ran under an Alpine downhill race, a slalom, and two ski-jumping events. The voice grew louder as a man went down and rolled over. His skis broke up. He looked badly injured.

"Recognize anything?" Don asked Elissa.

"Not yet. Is there ice-skating later? I pictured ice-skating."

"Nope, that's it." The reel was over. "Don't take it

hard. This was just a warm-up so you'd get used to the procedure. I didn't really expect you to pick up anything." He flicked on the light switch. "Shouldn't you deliver that order, Billy?"

"I guess so," Billy said. He seemed relieved that Elissa hadn't hit the targets. He rose, got into the long overcoat, and reached for the cardboard box. But before he touched it, he let out a screech and crumpled. While Elissa watched in shock, he writhed about like a hooked fish. His eyes stared; his lips were snarling.

"Go get help!" Don said. He pushed a chair out of the way and knelt beside Billy. "Try the rooms along the corridor."

Elissa ran out of the office, through the waiting room, and into the corridor. The first room was the teaching assistants' office, and she found Al sorting art prints into envelopes for dream experiments.

"Something's wrong with Billy! He's in Don's office."

Al dropped the prints and ran through the waiting room.

For a moment Elissa lingered in the corridor, struck by the sense that she had lived through the scene before. The bare floors, the look of the walls, the sense of urgency. Had it been in Manhattan State or when one of Sam's drunks had landed him in the Florida Keys Hospital? Still trying to match up the feeling with memory, she crossed the waiting room and approached Don's office.

Billy was still on the floor but he was calm now. Al was kneeling beside him. Don was taking his gold pen from Billy's mouth.

"He's okay now. Didn't bite his tongue. He'll be groggy for a while though. Let's lie him down on the waiting room sofa. Take a look—has he got his Dilantin?"

As Al searched Billy's pockets, Don glanced up and saw Elissa. "Epileptic seizure. Grand mal. Luckily, he's not getting them so often."

She was still staring, putting together the corridor, Al running, the boy jumping around the floor as if he was being electrocuted. "I saw it!" she said. "When I was trying to see into the future."

Don's gaze sharpened. "Did we tape it?"

As she nodded, Al said, "Here's a bottle. It's the Dilantin."

Don stood up. "Can you get him to the sofa? I want to play that tape."

"It's Billy all right. The corridor, the boy, the seizure," Don said as her recorded voice finished. He pushed the stop button and regarded the little cassette with awe.

Elissa shook her head slowly. It seemed impossible that she had seen Billy's grand mal attack before he had even arrived at the psi lab. And yet she had. The boy on the floor, jumping around as if he was being electrocuted—who could it be but Billy? If only she'd seen Steve's murder as clearly.

"You don't realize how remarkable it is, your first time out," Don started, then lapsed into silence, his eyes growing thoughtful. "You were right on target with Billy. I wonder if your other picture was precognitive. I don't see how, though. A golden man and books and flowers—"

"A bowl of flowers," said Elissa. She plumbed her memory for more than was on the tape, things she had *seen* but in her drowsiness had not bothered to mention. The temple had looked—"Japanese. It was a Japanese sort of temple."

"It doesn't make sense," Don muttered. He replayed that portion of the tape, then tipped back his chair and laced his fingers behind his head. As he thought, he leaned perilously backward. "Golden man, books, flowers, temple."

"And ice-skating."

"Skating," Don murmured. He looked up in excitement, then caught at his desk to keep his chair from tipping backward. "The gold statue of Prometheus! Books—there's a bookshop. And a Japanese airline ticket office. They always decorate their window. A picture of that temple in Kyoto and a flower arrangement! It's Rockefeller Center!"

"And those pools that run down the center island!" She stopped abruptly in dismay. "They were full of blood!"

"Some kind of violence, it looks like. A jealous lover shooting his girl friend? No, scarcely whole pools of blood in one girl friend. A sniper maybe? On top of a setback, taking pot shots? Did you see anything to indicate a sniper? People hitting the ground? A SWAT team?"

She tried to calm her mind and disregard the sense of pressure. But knowing she might prevent a tragedy made it harder. "Concentrate," she ordered herself, but her mind only blurred with the effort.

"There was just the golden man and the temple and flowers. Then the pools of blood." Suddenly she felt sick. "And the leg. The man's leg. But there wasn't any body." She looked at him. "How could a sniper do that?"

"He couldn't." His brows drew together. "But a bomb could. Maybe a bombing. A terrorist bombing!"

She looked grave.

"Okay, a bombing then. But when?" he asked. "Think back, Elissa. Any clue to when?"

"It was night, I'm pretty certain. I think there was night lighting."

"Tonight? Tomorrow night? What night?"

She thought frantically. But she came up with no more. After a moment she shook her head.

"We've got to know. We can't just tell the Bomb Squad—"

"We can't tell them. I mean, it was just a picture, I can't swear it's going to happen."

But he wasn't listening. He had pulled a Manhattan classified directory from the bottom drawer of his desk and was leafing through it.

"Air—Air Conditioning—Air Lines." He picked up his phone, dialed, and in a moment said, "Japan Air Lines? Do you have a bowl of flowers in your window? And a picture of a temple?" He listened intently. "I'm teaching a course on window decoration. How often do you change your display? I want to send my students to look before you change it." He listened a moment, said, "Thank you, miss," and hung up.

"It's the Kyoto temple and a bowl of dwarf iris. But they're changing it tonight. That means it's just about to happen."

"We can't be sure. It's probably a crime if you're wrong with the Bomb Squad."

He paid no attention. Jumping up, he strode through the waiting room and shouted down the corridor, "Say, Al, who's that cop you play handball with?"

Al poked his head out the door of the teaching assistants' office. "At the Y? Mike Hanley."

"Isn't he with the Bomb Squad?"

"Yeah. You ought to hear his stories."

"I've got him a new one. Call him! Rockefeller Center is going to be bombed!"

By six thirty that evening the smell of cooking shrimp gumbo was mixing with the scent of Hawaiian grass in Don's Village apartment on Charles Street. The sound of Stevie Wonder rose above Don's voice calling out orders to Al and Billy for finding the parts to the dinner table— two wooden trestles purloined from some long-ago street barricade, laid over by planks, but oddly grand in effect when Jenny threw the white tablecloth over it. The sound was shattering but the neighbors were apparently used to it. Anyway, Don's upstairs neighbors, two pretty girls from an ad agency, were helping Don make the gumbo in the kitchen.

Occasionally they wandered through pouring rosé into the glasses, offering tokes, and changing records on the stereo, which rambled about the apartment in parts. The whole place had the air of an experimental theater. Lamps divided into sections; a Navaho rug was pushed to one side, baring the hardwood flooring, which was being refinished. Someone had left an unfinished mural of an abstract bird on one wall. There were no chairs or sofa. Elissa lounged on a giant pillow she had taken from a multicolored heap in one corner. She hadn't been smoking and was only playing with her wine, but the grassy effluvia combined with Stevie Wonder had made her feel strangely disconnected. Then as the more muted strains of Chuck Mangione came from the stereo, her thoughts began settling again on the Bomb Squad.

Captain Hanley had been hard to convince. A hunch from a psi lab hadn't seemed good enough to send out four men and demolition equipment. As she'd listened to Al's side of the conversation, Elissa's face had flamed at what she gathered were sardonic remarks about the cure for girl psychics. Then Don had grabbed the phone.

"You send them out for every nut who makes a threatening phone call. What if I told you I'd planted a bomb to revenge the passenger pigeon? You'd empty the place in ten minutes."

After a struggle Captain Hanley had grudgingly consented.

What bothered Elissa was the silence since then. They hadn't heard that a bomb had been found or that it hadn't. And glancing at her wristwatch, she saw that two hours had passed since Al's call to Hanley. She began to wish she hadn't gotten into it, hadn't gone to the psi lab in the first place, hadn't told Jenny about her first vision, most importantly, that she had kept Steve out of it. If the police investigated, and they probably would, with somebody calling out the Bomb Squad, Steve might hear of it and dislike her claiming to be psychic. And she hadn't wanted, she remembered, to be hypnotized. She had dimly felt it was dangerous to submit her will to another person. How did she know she hadn't been given some posthypnotic suggestion? Perhaps, she thought wildly, to decoy Steve to his death. Though Al and Jenny had been present, so it couldn't have been done then. Except, what did she know about Al and Jenny really? That Jenny was born and raised in Brooklyn, liked baroque music, and was an editor's assistant. And that Al had been a basketball center at college and now was a teaching assistant. They might be anything—political activists or foreign agents or even terrorists. For that matter, what did she know about Don himself?

Stop! she ordered herself sternly. It was all crazy, thinking they might be giving her hypnotic suggestions or be enemy agents.

"It's not like he was already President," Billy said, breaking into her fevered thoughts. He had recovered from his seizure and was standing next to her, a bit shaky. "I mean if Cameron were really President—but I don't think spies go after Governors."

She looked up at him, astonished.

His pale urchin's face grew hopeful. "Did I get it?"

"But that's—invading my privacy. Do you always know what people are thinking?"

"No. I can only do it sometimes. If I'm, like, in tune with the person." He plucked a pillow from the pile and joined her. "And they usually have to be upset. I think it makes them broadcast stronger."

"But if you read minds, why don't you tune in on the bombers?"

"I have to know the person. It's like a blind man feeling with his fingers. I kind of scan for the wave length. And I can't do it often really. I think we must have a lot in common. Being psi, we've got the same sort of problems."

Suddenly Don shouted, "Turn off that music!"

He was in the bedroom, between them and the kitchen. Elissa supposed it was a bedroom. All it contained was a king-sized mattress and a packing crate topped with a

TV set. Don and the ad girls had wandered in from the kitchen to watch the set. The anchor man emerged faintly from Chuck Mangione. Elissa scrambled to her feet to switch off the stereo, but Al did it first.

". . . The men who were killed were both members of the Bomb Squad," the anchor man said clearly. "Traffic is being diverted from Fifth Avenue between Forty-ninth and Fifty-sixth streets."

As he moved to conditions in the Middle East, Don turned off the set.

Elissa and he regarded one another in somber silence.

"How many were killed?" she asked.

"Two. Both members of the Bomb Squad. They'd already evacuated everybody from the Channel Gardens. It went off while they were defusing. It was a time bomb set for midnight."

At the look on her face he said, "You can't always avert it."

"If it had gone off at midnight, nobody would have been there."

"Sure they would," Billy said. He was standing behind them, listening. "There are always people at Rockefeller Center."

"Not those men from the Bomb Squad. They wouldn't have been there. I *caused* that," she said. "I got them killed!"

Chapter 11

Captain Hanley might have an affable side that Al had seen playing handball. But for Elissa's interview next morning, he was dour and clearly suspicious of psychic girls who sent his men to their deaths.

He asked, "How did you hit on Rockefeller Center?"

She wished he had let Don in to explain about brain waves so it would sound more scientific, but he was interviewing them separately. Don had had to wait outside.

Locking her fingers in her lap, she looked about for inspiration. But she found none in the bare metal desk or the walls without pictures. There wasn't even a window. It was like being inside a steel locker.

She said, "They wanted to test if I could see into the future. So Professor Young hooked me up to a brain wave machine and I got these pictures."

"What pictures?" asked Captain Hanley.

"Ice-skaters and a gold man and flowers."

His gaze was bleak with disbelief.

"I didn't actually see them," she hurriedly said. "It was just in my mind, like you do when you daydream."

His look said he wasn't given to daydreaming.

"I saw pools of blood and—" She hesitated, knowing it was one of his men she was describing. "A man's leg. Don—Professor Young—thought it sounded like Rockefeller Center."

His face told her Don would have to do some explaining. "How did he know it was a bombing?"

"The blood in the pools in the Channel Gardens and, I guess, the leg."

He pulled out a desk drawer, made an entry in a notebook, and slid the drawer shut. "How did you meet Professor Young?"

"Al Martin lives in my apartment building. He's his teaching assistant." She hoped he might be softened by the mention of his handball partner, but he didn't show any sign of softening.

"Why did he test you? Do you often have these hunches?"

She reflected quickly on what she could tell him. Nothing about Steve, of course; that was out of the question. But the man in the elevator was unwise, too. She was in trouble enough with the Bomb Squad without taking on Homicide. She decided to beg the question. "I got a high score on a card test."

He looked bored and she hoped Don wouldn't go into more detail. Then he reopened the desk and consulted his notebook. "Your father's a writer."

She nodded, and he said, "Sam Blake."

From his tone he might as well have added, "Dangerous radical." As she made the connection between radicals and terrorists, her heart sank. If they brought Sam into it, there was no telling where his joy in being thought dangerous might lead.

The phone rang and Captain Hanley seized it. "I told you no calls!" Then a strange expression touched his face.

After a moment he said, "I see, sir." While he listened, his gaze wandered to Elissa and he fixed her with nerve-racking attention. Perhaps, she thought, Don was already being interrogated and had come out with all her visions. "She's in my office now," said Hanley. Then, "Yes, sir." He rose and gave the phone to Elissa. "It's the Governor." Elissa raised the receiver with apprehension.

"I hear you called out the Bomb Squad," said Steve.

"No!" she cried in dismay.

"The Bomb Squad says you did. The police commissioner just called me here in Madison. He was checking your story about being one of my staff photographers."

She gave a small moan of misery. "Don must have told them. I'm sorry."

"Who's Don?"

"Professor Young. He teaches psychology and runs the psi lab."

"Psi is short for psychic? And he's got you predicting bombings?"

"I did that on my own. I had this dream. And Don thought we ought to warn them." Perhaps, she thought, this was the time to tell him about his own death. She had foretold a bomb and it had gone off, so maybe he'd listen without jumping to the conclusion that she was unbalanced. But before she could come out with it, he sighed.

"All we need is a psychic staff photographer mixing it up in terrorist bombings."

As she flinched, Captain Hanley mercifully left the office.

"Listen, Elissa," Steve said with patience, "keep away from that psychic professor."

"Okay," she said, trying to sound as if it didn't matter.

"So far we've kept your part of it from the press. The police commissioner isn't any happier than we are about having them say his Bomb Squad was acting on a psychic tip. So he's cooperating. But if there's a leak—" He sighed again and said, "You'd better come out here where we can cover you if they do pick up a rumor."

"Right," she said. And more softly, "I'm sorry."

"Don't even go home. You can buy clothes when you get here. When you leave the police station, take a cab directly to La Guardia. There'll be a ticket at American Airlines. Catch the next plane for Madison, Wisconsin. Look around at the airport. You'll be met."

The day after the Wisconsin and New York primaries, Cherry's bar was nearly empty. Jack Frost presided over Happy Hour with only two customers, the blonde with the crazy blue eyes and a gray-haired man in a worn tweed jacket. Jack set a bowl of popcorn beside the man's rye and water. "How's the work going?"

The man shrugged.

Jack nodded respectfully. Nowadays, Tom Barton wrote plays that never came to production. But in the golden age of Hollywood, he had written a motion picture that Jack still remembered. It still struck Jack as a marvel that the author of a famous movie that he had seen as a boy should be, for all intents, a friend. Barton talked to Jack—about pollution, city violence, oil depletion—like an equal, and Jack treated Barton as if he were a kind of tutor for still greater marvels to come. He approached their sessions with care, studying *Time* or *Newsweek*, and made his opening like a chess play.

"Now what do you make of Cameron's chances?"

"Hard to tell," said Barton. "Of course, he carried New York. You'd expect that. But the loss in Wisconsin was a blow."

"I think he'll win in Pennsylvania."

"Carter might take Pennsylvania."

"Well, Ohio and California—"

"I don't see how you can figure California."

A big Irishman in a green guard's uniform entered. Jack

gave no sign of noticing his arrival and continued the discussion with Barton. When Francis began fidgeting on his barstool, Jack made a show of surprise and moved to serve him.

"Hello, Francis," he said with cool courtesy. "I didn't see you."

Francis looked at him mutely. The long, heavy face seemed to be gathering courage.

"What'll it be?" asked Jack. He didn't ask, The usual?

"Long time no see," said Francis with the lightness of an elephant trying to juggle an acorn.

"Really? I hadn't noticed."

Francis took a great breath. "I'm here to apologize," he blurted. "I was taken with the drink that day. I hardly knew what I was saying."

"You didn't say anything I recall," said Jack coldly.

Sweat began to mottle Francis's forehead. " 'Tis a terrible weakness, the drink. You shouldn't hold it against me. If you knew sometimes how I struggled—"

Jack shrugged.

"I didn't mean it, you know, the way it sounded. Sure in my right mind I know you wasn't trying to get me drunk. Nor that madness either about the board meeting."

Jack arched his brows as if he didn't remember.

"Getting me drunk so you could take my place the night of the board meeting," said Francis helpfully.

"Oh that? I thought that was a joke." Jack smiled. His smile looked so easy that Francis smiled hesitantly.

" 'Twas all it was indeed, a joke. You wouldn't be holding a grudge about a joke now?"

"It had slipped my mind," said Jack lightly.

Francis looked relieved. "Shake on it?" he asked, extending his palm. But Jack had already begun slicing up oranges for old-fashioneds and both his hands were busy.

"When you're through there, I'd like a draft beer," Francis said, reverting to his former humble manner. And then, as Jack didn't show signs of hearing: "The Governor didn't even make it that night. He had to go to Wisconsin."

Jack shrugged.

"If you want to meet him so much, maybe we can work out something," said Francis wretchedly. It seemed to be wrenched out of him by the mortal loneliness of a man who has almost made a friend and sees him slipping away.

But Jack's eyes suddenly shifted color so that a greenish light seemed to flame behind them. "Will you take your museum and stick it up your ass, Francis?"

Francis stared at him, flabbergasted.

"There's no problem about me seeing Cameron." Jack's voice rose. "And I'm sick of your badgering to move in with me. I'm telling you to quit coming in here. If I see you again, I'll throw you into the fucking street."

He grabbed up a knife, strode down the bar, and fell to slashing cartons of whiskey open as Francis watched him in astonishment. For some minutes there was silence, except for the sound of ripping cardboard. Pale with mortification, Francis finally slid off his barstool and left.

Soon Mr. Barton glanced at his wristwatch. He made a display of being late, said, "See you tomorrow, Jack," and departed.

Only the blonde lingered, her eyes on Jack in the bar mirror as she sipped at her martini. After a bit Jack began setting out whiskey bottles. He seemed calmer, though his hands still trembled

She asked, "What was all that in aid of?"

"Goddamn old queen."

"No kidding! He proposition you?"

He shrugged and poured her a dividend.

"No wonder you got sore," she said.

In the companionable silence that followed, Jack put away the bottles. By the time he was finished, he was even shaking his head ruefully.

At last he turned back to the bar, his equanimity restored. His hostly duties seemed to demand that he mend the fabric of the evening. "Hey, you know who came in last night? I meant to tell you. Van Allen."

"Walter?" She looked disbelieving. "But I was here!"

"He came in after you left. It must have been about ten thirty."

She still gazed at him doubtfully. "How did he look?"

"Looked fine. Suntanned. Got himself one of those Acapulco suntans."

She smiled at the persuasive picture. "Good old Walter. Did his heiress toss him out?"

"No. That's all fine. Matter of fact, he was on his way to Spain to stay at her castle."

"When is he going?"

"He went this morning. Said he'd write when he knows the address."

"But didn't he used to live there?"

"That's right." He seemed to consider. "Maybe she sold that and bought another. Now I look back, I think he mentioned it."

She frowned at her drink and he came closer to cheer her. "Tell you what. One of these days we'll run over together and surprise him. I'll get the tickets and we'll fly across for a weekend, stay at a grand hotel and all that."

In spite of herself, she smiled. "Did you buy a ticket on the sweepstakes?"

"You'll see," he said with an air of mystery.

"You've found another fortune teller!" For some time they had been trading astrologists, Tarot readers, psychic advisers.

"I'm going to move in high circles." The words had the queer, grandiose ring of private reflection. "My fortunes are verging on change."

He closed the bar at two, washed up, totaled the night's receipts, and left the money in the office safe for Cherry, an elderly blonde in a Mary Pickford hairstyle who was driven around to her three bars every morning by a black chauffeur in white livery. Then he exchanged his barman's coat for a black leather jacket, set the burglar alarm, and let himself out on a deserted Fifty-fourth Street.

He strode across town, keeping a watch for muggers, although in his black leather he himself caused one wary stroller to cross the street. At Eighth Avenue he stopped at an all-night delicatessen for barbecued chicken and coleslaw, and proceeded down the street to the door beside the pawnshop. He unlocked the door and carried his purchases upstairs.

In his apartment he turned the two locks and went directly through the living room into the kitchen. Removing his jacket, he stood at the sink and bolted the chicken and coleslaw. Then he washed his hands, took up a dustcloth, returned to the living room, and polished the spotless glass-topped table. Next he went to the bedroom and from the nightstand beneath the Steve Cameron poster, he took a package. Bearing it back to the living room, he turned on the lamp behind the sofa, switched off the wall lights, and drew out a paperback dictionary, a ball-point pen, and a tablet marked Linen Writing Paper. He laid them before him, then lit a cigarette and sat staring at a pristine ashtray. At last he lifted the tablet's cover, picked up the ball-point, and began to write.

Dear Governor Cameron,
    Congratulations on your New York victory.

He frowned, picked up the dictionary, and checked the spelling of victory, but the frown continued to pucker the scar above his eyebrow. He ripped off the page, balled it, and started again.

Dear Steve Cameron,
    You are about to make a new friend.

* * *

On Friday evening before the Memorial Day weekend, Jay Dolan rang Elissa at her apartment. "The car will pick you up at nine o'clock."

"But the flight leaves at eight!"

"It's been changed. We decided to take the press, so we're chartering."

It was already seven. She glanced at her bag, already packed. She supposed she was lucky she hadn't already gone downstairs to wait for the car, but there was no use pointing it out. Jay knew it already. They had managed to keep her part in the bombing from the press. Cued by the police commissioner, Captain Hanley had told them the Bomb Squad had been tipped off by the source they must protect while investigation continued. But Jay had not forgiven her for nearly causing trouble. Harassing her with minor mix-ups was one of his methods to try to make her leave the staff.

"Okay," she said, "nine o'clock."

He wouldn't let her hang up peaceably, however. "The press is going to be aboard," he repeated. "So watch your step."

"I will," she said, trying to sidestep what she sensed was coming.

But he insisted on spelling it out: "Don't start talking about second sight or bombings."

She wanted to protest. He was being insulting, treating her like a hysterical girl who was trying to catch the limelight. But she knew it was part of his baiting, trying to make her lose her head and quit. She forced back the protest and simply said, "Don't worry, Jay. I won't talk to the press," and hung up.

Afterward she walked to the window. As she stared at the chimney pot silhouetted against the Village sunset, she returned again to Madison, Wisconsin, reliving the first awful moments when she'd arrived at Steve's hotel suite.

* * *

Steve was in shirt sleeves, lying on the sofa; Jay was standing with his back to a window, the light behind him as if it truly were an interrogation.

"Just how did you get involved in this mess?" Jay demanded.

Steve raised his hand to Jay in a calming gesture but Jay didn't see it; as he glared at her, the cigarette between his lips spilled ashes down his shirtfront.

"They were testing me for precognition," she began with apprehension.

"Who's 'they'?" Jay interrupted.

"Professor Young, the man who runs the psi lab."

"Why was he testing you? Where did you meet him?"

"One of my neighbors is his teaching assistant." She thought quickly. It was clearly no time to bring up the man in the elevator. "They were just looking for people to test and I agreed."

"You shouldn't agree to crazy propositions. Not while you're with a presidential candidate. This man is probably looking for publicity—"

"He's not!" she flared. "He's a professor! A famous parapsychologist!"

Steve sat up and ran his hands through his hair in a smoothing gesture. "Okay, Jay, quit lighting matches under her toenails."

He held out his hand and she came to him and sat beside him on the sofa.

"Look, Elissa, you're part of my team, and right now we're in a tough ball game."

He pressed her hand. "We'll win in New York. But Wisconsin and Pennsylvania are chancy. Brown is coming into the race from California. And then there's Church— It looks like a dogfight."

She didn't know where he was headed, but she nodded.

"If the press says we're gazing into crystal balls and getting mixed up in terrorist bombings—"

"I couldn't help it!"

"Think about the bombing, Elissa. They'd ask how you really knew, who your associates were. They'd dig up your father—"

"But it just came into my mind the way a dream does." And at the disbelief in his eyes, "What about that dream I had in Miami? Where I saw how many delegates—"

"God save us all," Jay exploded. "She really believes it!"

"That was a coincidence," said Steve gravely. "And if it wasn't—believe me, Elissa, this is no time for us to get into it."

She sat very still for a moment. She had almost come out with the draft riots, the rape-murder, even his own death. But now she saw he was so focused on the election that he wouldn't listen. Nothing mattered but Wisconsin, New York, and Pennsylvania. If he felt she was endangering their chances, she realized he would protect the rest of his staff by dismissing her.

"I understand. I didn't think," she said at last. "I'm sorry."

Jay started to speak but Steve frowned. "We've all said enough. Okay, Elissa, we have to work. You'd better go now."

Jay still looked unyielding as a statue as she left.

As she stood at the window watching the gathering dusk in the Village, she considered the six weeks since then and she felt like crying. Besides the constant travel, the work itself, and the lack of sleep, there had been a sudden run of political losses. After the New York win, Wisconsin and Pennsylvania had gone to Carter. Then six more states went to Brown and Church. The voters seemed beguiled by fresh faces and there was press speculation that Steve had come out too soon, that he should have waited for a convention draft. Facing the press on television and in his speeches at political dinners, Steve maintained an easy confidence. He cheerfully claimed that with the Carter thrust broken, he only had to carry three states more to win the Democratic nomination.

But could he carry them? New Jersey was a Cameron state. However, Ohio wasn't certain. And California could be a disaster. When only his staff was present, his face was strained and often downright grim.

After the scene with Steve and Jay in Madison, Elissa had wondered why Steve kept her on. Even in Miami he'd wanted to send her home to Key West, and he'd only brought her with him to keep her out of the newspapers during the bomb investigation. But once that was over, she felt she was only hanging on because Jay was waiting for her to make one more false step. And Steve? Steve was so harried, he seemed to forget her for days at a time.

She had seen him alone only at accidental moments, and almost at once they were interrupted by Jay Dolan with a new poll, an emergency problem with the media, a changed schedule. At Steve's look of exhaustion Elissa felt how pitilessly he was caught between Old Tom's pride and Jay's driving ambition, which daily seemed to grow more naked. Even Amanda's charms had been vanquished. She was on the press train, at the banquet table, in the audience, lovely as ever, as politely attentive, but there were no more traded glances or carefree banter. All point in life but politics was gone.

She stood at the window till the sunset had faded and the chimney pots were absorbed by darkness. When the knock came at her door, she hesitated because the downstairs buzzer hadn't warned her. But the knocking was insistent.

"Come on, Elissa, open up. Billy says you're in there." It was Don. As the racket increased, she switched on a lamp, went to the door, and Don strolled past her into her apartment, trailed by Billy. "Billy's like having a psychic bloodhound."

She smiled at Billy uncertainly, hoping he hadn't picked up her thoughts by the window. But she couldn't tell. His thin face simply looked embarrassed at being part of Don's invasion. She had been avoiding them all, even Al and Jenny, since the day in Madison. She had been out of town a lot, of course, and she had hoped that would explain it. Even today when Jenny had called to invite her to dinner, she had been able to say she was leaving for California. But Billy's expression told her the excuses had been useless. She had been keeping away from them and they knew.

"Elissa," Don said, "you've got to come back to the psi lab. It's vitally important."

All she could think to say was, "I can't."

"Is it Cameron? Did he tell you not to do it?"

Relieved to have it out in the open, she said, "He hated it so when I saw the bombing. I mean, be fair. If it got in the papers—"

" 'Psychic Aide to Presidential Candidate'? It does sound loopy," he admitted. "But why can't you quit? If you're not on his staff, if there's no connection—" He stopped as he saw her expression. "I see. It's love. You can't bring yourself to leave him."

She didn't answer.

"Listen, Elissa, the New York Premonitions Registry just got its first two warning dreams on Cameron."

Her sea-blue eyes widened as if he had struck her.

He said, "You see, the number of precognitions increases as the event gets closer. Remember I told you about the schoolchildren who were killed in the Aberfan slag slide? Of the thirty-five recorded predictions, eighteen were made within four days of the disaster."

"Are there always warnings?"

"Nearly always. Particularly for important things like plane crashes and assassinations. With somebody of Cameron's stature I'd say it was certain."

"And can they tell where it's going to happen?"

"Not precisely, because it's filtered through the dreamer's unconscious. That's why I had to see you. In both warning dreams the dreamers spoke of hills and water. Could you see out of doors in your own vision?"

"No. The suite doesn't have any windows. Just air conditioning."

He glanced at her suitcase. "Jenny said you're off to California."

She nodded.

"What do hills and water make you think of?"

Her gaze shadowed with understanding.

"Tell him to watch out in San Francisco," he said.

There were two pieces of mail in Jack Frost's mailbox, a copy of *Newsweek* and a letter from the Governor's office in Albany. He glanced at the *Newsweek* cover of Steve Cameron surrounded by crowds in Sacramento, captioned ON TO SAN FRANCISCO, then carried the letter back upstairs.

In his apartment, he bolted his door and slit open the letter carefully.

OFFICE OF THE GOVERNOR
Albany, N.Y.

May 28, 1976

Mr. Jack Frost
761 Eighth Avenue
New York, N.Y.

Dear Mr. Frost,

Thank you for your kind letter of support for my campaign for President.

I believe we can win the Democratic nomination and carry the nation with us to Washington.

With very best wishes,
Steve Cameron

SC/bk

He stood in the little kitchen, rereading the letter in disbelief. Then he crumpled the envelope and threw it into the garbage basket. He tore up the letter and tossed it after the envelope.

The electric wall clock was slightly out of line and without conscious intent he began to level it. But rage caught him like a wave and he wrenched the clock off the wall and hurled it after the letter. He stood thinking.

At last he moved to the cupboard and took down the American Express card, Van Allen's driver's license, and a folded wad of money.

Leaving his apartment, he went down the marble stairs and strode along Eighth Avenue to a pay phone booth. The directories had all been ripped from their chains, so he dialed Information.

When the airlines reservations clerk answered, he said, "I want a flight to San Francisco. Today."

Chapter 12

Elissa woke in Steve Cameron's suite at the Fairmont. It was still strange to her to share a bed, and she had slept lightly, waking half a dozen times and being careful when she turned not to disturb him, so that she wasn't really rested. Her mouth was dry from the vodka she had drunk about midnight and her cheeks and forehead felt slightly feverish. For a while she lay motionless beside him, hoping to go back to sleep, but there was too much daylight coming through the windows, and finally she rose and padded barefoot to the bathroom.

When she returned, he seemed to be dreaming. He frowned and moved his head in a harried manner, then flung himself to her side of the bed. She wondered if he would want her to wake him from the nightmare. Unsure, she put on her shirt, went to a bedroom window, and gazed down the hill of San Francisco at the bay.

But the view could not hold her attention. Her thoughts kept circling the man on the bed. She wondered if his dream was triggered by present or past troubles, by the campaign or painful memories. Standing by the window, she returned to last night.

They had flown in from a two-day tour of northern California in time for Steve to make a television appearance and go on to a rally at the University of California at Berkeley. At the last minute Jay had told her that another photographer would be going with them, so she found a twenty-four-hour photographic service and took them her day's pictures. She went back to the hotel, gave her laundry to the valet, then washed her hair and called Room Service for a steak and salad. When her order arrived, she turned on the television set and got into bed with her tray and had her dinner while she watched Steve's interview. He had looked haggard when she'd last seen him at the airport, but on the television screen he seemed young and vigorous and confident. She'd seen him do it before, tap into some inner reservoir of strength for important appearances, so she wasn't really surprised; she only wondered how long he could continue without a break for rest. But that thought disturbed her so she got up and switched to the rerun of a documentary on the animals of the High Sierras.

After the documentary she watched an old Sherlock Holmes movie, and somewhere in the middle she must have fallen asleep. Then her phone was ringing, and she found herself still sitting up with two pillows behind her and the television playing. She glanced at her watch and saw it was after eleven.

It was Steve. "You sound sleepy," he accused. "Did I wake you?"

"I was just watching an old movie." She glanced at the screen and saw that Basil Rathbone had been replaced by a blonde in a red sequined gown that plunged in front almost to her navel. It appeared to be a talk show. "I guess the movie went off and I didn't notice."

"Do you have the pictures you took in Stockton?"

"I dropped them off tonight to be developed." And as he made a frustrated noise, she said, "No, wait! I did that before we left Sacramento! I probably still have them. I haven't had a chance to give them to Bob Spears yet." Bob Spears was their California coordinator.

"Could you rustle them up for me?"

"Tonight?"

"Sure. The evening is young yet."

She looked at her watch again but she'd read it correctly the first time. The Berkeley rally must have recharged him. "I'll be there in five minutes."

She got out of bed and looked at herself in the mirror above the bureau. After a moment she rooted in her attaché case till she found the pictures. Moving swiftly, she stepped into her slacks, buttoned up a fresh shirt, and slipped on a pair of espadrilles.

As he opened the door to his suite, Steve took the sheaf of pictures she had shot in Stockton, and shuffled through them. "I told one of the State Senators I'd see he got his picture." It was such a lame excuse, they both smiled. He handed her a drink he had waiting for her on the coffee table. "It's been a bitch of a trip. No time to do what I wanted." Suddenly she felt wonderful; her smile widened.

He took her free hand and led her to the sofa. "You look better. No more sleepwalking?" And as she shook her head: "No more nightmares?"

"No more nightmares."

"And I hope no visions."

A cloud passed over her joy at his mention of visions. She'd been wondering how to warn him about San Francisco, but now she shrank from the chance of ruining their private evening.

"Oh no," he said, seeing the change in her expression.

"I didn't do this one myself. It's the New York Premonitions Registry."

"What the hell's that?" And when she'd told him: "I thought you promised you'd quit seeing that professor."

"He came by before I went to the airport. He told me to warn you the Premonitions Bureau was getting assassination dreams for a place with hills and water. It sounded like San Francisco."

His face darkened. "I'm supposed to listen to a bunch of dreamers?"

"But if it's true?" she asked. "It could prevent your death!"

"How? What could I do about it? Stop going out in public? I'd lose California."

As she stared at him in disbelief, he lowered his gaze to the ice cubes in his vodka.

"Isn't dying more important than an election?" she asked.

He considered. "It sounds strange, but dying becomes irrelevant. It's like taking an express train. Once you're rolling, you don't get off till the train stops."

"Don't or can't?"

He hesitated. "It's no longer a personal decision. You make too many commitments."

"No matter what the ride will do to you?"

"It doesn't look like it." He sighed. "Neither to you nor to anyone else."

It occurred to her that he was speaking of his marriage, and she remembered the lovely young woman she'd seen in the Key West boutique in her pink shirt.

"You mean Cathy?" she asked, and when he nodded: "I saw her once but I never met her. What was she like?"

"Shy. Pretty. Easily frightened. She needed assurance. And affection—more than I had time to give her." He added: "You've probably picked up the gossip—she started drinking."

At the pain in his voice she felt an answering pain. "It's hard when they drink."

He remembered Sam then. "You had your father, didn't you?"

"He's stopped now. But not till last year."

"And your mother? I always wondered. Did she die or did she leave him?"

"She . . . left. But not because of his drinking." She hesitated again and then blurted, "She's spent years in mental institutions. We thought the drugs had made her psychotic. Now it turns out she was really psychic." He frowned but she hurried on. "She saw things that were going to happen. Don says that happens to a lot of people, and they end up in asylums. A boy at the lab came out of Rockland."

"Elissa!" He set down his drink and faced her, his blue eyes penetrating. "I couldn't understand why you believed this junk so quickly. But don't you see, it was your mother's illness. You couldn't accept it."

"She wasn't ill! Don says—"

"Somebody ought to wring Don's neck, too. Elissa, this stuff will destroy you. You've got to come back to the real world."

They were both silent, each stubbornly holding to his own position. Then under the lever of his disapproval her nerve failed and she yielded. "Okay."

"I'm sorry. I know you've been under pressure," he said more gently. As she sat motionless, he smoothed her shining hair with his palm, then took the drink from her and set it on the coffee table. "This is real," he said, and kissed her. "Let's not waste a real night."

As she stood by the window in the morning light, looking out at the bay below them, the phone rang and she moved to catch it before it woke him. Then she remembered he was the widower Governor and a woman's voice was not supposed to answer so early. Helplessly, she watched him roll over. He put out a hand and felt for the phone.

"Hello," he said hoarsely, and after a moment, "Won't it wait, Jay? For God's sake!"

He rubbed a hand across his forehead as he listened. Then he made a rueful face at Elissa.

She took her slacks from a chair and began stepping into them. As she was hopping about, pulling on her loafers, he hung up. "Jay's got himself another crisis," he said apologetically.

She reached for her shoulder bag.

"Elissa, I'm sorry."

She kissed her fingers to him and went quickly out the door.

As she let herself into her room, her phone was ringing. The sound had a queer urgency in a strange city at that time in the morning, and she picked up the instrument, hoping nothing had happened to Sam. But it was, of all people, Billy.

"I hope it's not too early in California," he said, suddenly diffident at having reached her. "I guess there's a big time difference."

"Three hours. But I was already up," she said, wondering why he'd phoned her.

"It was a hassle getting your number out of Cameron's headquarters. I had to tell them I was your cousin and give them a lot of emergency jazz. If they should ask—"

"Don't worry."

A pause followed while she waited.

"How's the trip going?" he asked her finally.

"Fine. We've been to Stockton and Sacramento and San Jose." She stopped. "Oh. Do you mean about the hills and water? Has Don heard anything else?"

"Nothing like that. I just wondered, well, how you were." He sounded embarrassed and her bewilderment increased.

"I'm all right," she told him doubtfully.

"That's good," he said. "Glad to hear it's going okay.

Sorry to bother you calling so early. Take it easy now."
And he hung up.

She stood at the nightstand puzzling over why he had
called her. The underlying tone, she felt, had been concern. Perhaps he hadn't said more because he didn't want
to alarm her. But *she* was the one who had precognitive
visions, not Billy. Billy's extrasensory strength was
telepathy. Then suddenly she knew. He had picked up
her thoughts the way he had the night in Don's apartment.
He had tuned in on her feelings when she was with Steve.
He was probably worried because he realized now she
was in so deeply.

"Can I help you?" the operator asked and she saw that
she still held the disconnected instrument.

"No. Sorry."

Her cheeks were flaming as she hung up the phone.

The rest of Steve's day was tightly scheduled: interviews, two luncheon speeches, a trip to the Muir Woods,
and late in the afternoon a motorcade.

Steve was riding in the Mayor's open car for the
motorcade. Five cars back Elissa was taking random shots
of the crowds they were passing on Bush Street—a tense
young man with an anti-Cameron placard, a tired child
riding its father's shoulders, a beaming matron carrying
a bag of groceries. The others in her car were strangers,
college students from the San Francisco headquarters, and
she had no talent for quick intimacy with strangers. It
was easier to take pictures and pretend to be working.

Suddenly there were rapid explosions.

She had a blurred impression of startled faces turning,
a running Secret Service man, the girl beside her diving
to the car floor.

She sat paralyzed as her world fragmented. A bearded
boy in her car cried, "Oh God!" A man on Bush Street
coolly pointed his movie camera toward Steve's lead car.

An old man in a grocer's apron crossed himself. A small boy smiled and waved a flag on a stick.

Then their driver said, "We're crossing Grant Street!"

The bearded boy quit saying "Oh God!" He laughed and touched the shoulder of the girl on the car floor. "Get up, Helen! It's just Grant Street."

"What's Grant Street?" Elissa whispered.

"Chinatown. It's firecrackers!"

Relief poured through her. Her heart began to beat again, then suddenly was pounding wildly.

They were nearly to City Hall before she remembered the Premonitions Bureau. Their dreamers had seen Steve shot in a place of hills and water. Don had feared it would happen in San Francisco. And it *had*. Shots had rung out on a hill above the bay. The crowd had turned toward Steve while fear moved through them like wind rippling through sea grass. That was what the dreamers had picked up. She tried to recall what Don had told her about psi fields that sent copies back faster than the originals traveled. It had actually happened. The flaw was in interpretation: The shots were only firecrackers; Steve's death no more than an illusion.

It was true that her own vision of his death still lay in the future. But Don had said there would be more predictions as the event drew nearer. So with the danger over in San Francisco, Steve was safe until they had new warnings.

She relaxed, talked with the bearded boy and Helen, and took pictures of the City Hall ceremony. For a brief moment, as the ceremony ended and while the Secret Service men were breaking a way for Steve to his car, he turned and sought her eyes, freighting the look with meaning. She guessed he was acknowledging that firecrackers sounded like shots and that she had warned him of the hills and water.

It relieved her to know he wasn't so scornful anymore of premonitions.

She coasted through the rest of the afternoon with a sense of loosening tension. It was only when she got back to the hotel that she realized how severely the firecrackers had shocked her. Leaving the car, she knew she was exhausted, and glanced at her watch to see how much time she had before Steve's television appearance that evening. She decided she could have a shower, a quick nap, and a hamburger.

She was crossing the lobby when she saw the tall, fair man with the scar that puckered one eyebrow. His expression was clear and blandly pleasant as he watched Steve pass with the crowd of staff and Secret Service men. In simple reflex she raised her camera, and he was too absorbed in following Steve's progress to notice that she took his picture. When Steve's elevator door closed, he watched the floor levels as it rose to the staff floor.

When he strolled to the elevator bank, she had a panicky moment. She couldn't raise an alarm because a man had entered an elevator. And yet, it looked as though he was stalking Steve. It couldn't all be coincidence—seeing him at Chadwyck, then the night of the Florida primary, and now in San Francisco. As he stepped into a waiting elevator, she hurried across the lobby and stepped in beside him. The door closed and the elevator rose.

She tried to guess if he placed her from their meeting at Chadwyck. But if he did, he didn't betray the recognition. His face was impersonally pleasant.

"What floor?" he asked.

"Top, please," she said, not wanting to betray the Cameron staff floor.

He pushed the top button and she saw that he had already pressed the button for the floor above Steve's. So he hadn't planned on going to Steve's floor. Of course, an assassin would probably know it was guarded by

Secret Service men. He would wait his chance when Steve was going in or out.

"Don't miss the Muir Woods," he suddenly told her.

She was startled. They had toured there today. If Jack Frost had also been there, he might have seen her in Steve's party. But would he play games if he were bent on assassination?

They passed the staff floor, stopped on the floor above, and the elevator door slid open.

"You take it easy now," he said as he stepped out.

She knew no more than she had in the lobby. She didn't even know if he was staying at the Fairmont or was only reconnoitering. On impulse she pressed the button for the next level.

On the floor above she hurried along the corridor to the fire door, ran down a flight of stairs, and cautiously looked out.

Jack Frost was entering a room down the hallway. As he glanced about him, she drew back into the shadow of the stairwell. She waited, but apparently he hadn't seen her. Then all at once she found her legs were trembling. She sank to a step and considered.

She tried to recall where past assassins had struck. JFK had been riding in a motorcade in Dallas. Robert Kennedy had been in a public hotel room. Martin Luther King had been shot on a motel balcony. George Wallace had been addressing a crowd. Lincoln had been killed in a theater. All of them were shot in public places.

Had a politician ever been killed in a bedroom? Marat, she vaguely recalled, had been stabbed in his bath, and in those days baths possibly were set up in bedrooms. Today though, with the Secret Service, it seemed unlikely.

Yet she had seen Steve killed in a bedroom. And her psi ability had been proven. She had seen a future rape-murder and she'd seen a future bombing.

She tried to imagine how Jack Frost could get into Steve's bedroom. Perhaps if he dressed as a waiter delivering an order— Were the waiters cleared each time? she wondered. And what about bellhops and hotel repairmen? Although the warning would sound peculiar now that Steve thought the Premonitions Bureau's caution had been defused and the danger was over, she would have to tell him about her own vision of his death in the museum. Before, his disapproval had blocked her, but he had himself experienced the firecrackers. That should help him believe she'd seen the Rockefeller Center bombing. And between the two things, perhaps he would listen.

She rose, her pale hair swinging, and went down the fire stairs.

On the Cameron staff floor the fire door was locked but she knocked and the Secret Service man guarding it recognized her. "You should use the elevator."

"I rode past my floor."

He looked sternly at her but he let her enter. Then he watched her down the hall to Steve's door.

Steve was reading a new speech when he let her in. He smiled and shoved his tortoiseshell glasses back on his forehead. "I've got to admit I hit the dirt when those crackers went off on Bush Street."

"I'm glad it happened then because I've got another warning."

"Don't push your luck, girl. You'll overload me."

"I'm serious, Steve. The man I saw at Chadwyck is on the floor above you."

"What man?"

"I met a man on the grounds at Chadwyck. Later I saw him at the Florida primary."

"Look, love," he said, "I've got a talk tonight and a banquet."

"This is important, Steve! I saw him in the lobby. His name is Jack Frost and he has a scar above his eyebrow. He's following you around and he might be going to try to kill you."

He tossed the speech on the coffee table. "Look, Elissa,

there are political buffs just the way there are ballet buffs. Sometimes they follow candidates around the country."

"But I even got his room number. Couldn't you have the Secret Service talk to him? Maybe if he knew they were watching—"

"Oh God." He took hold of her shoulders and said with careful patience, "This is supposed to be a democratic country. The Secret Service can't intimidate a citizen because a girl saw him in a hotel."

"But he told me a pack of lies when he was trespassing at Chadwyck. And then I saw him in Miami. Now he's here."

He looked at her sharply. "Is this one of your premonitions?"

"No! I really saw him. They could search him. If they find a gun, they could hold him."

Jay rapped on the door and came in. He seemed harried and when he saw Elissa, he stopped in annoyance.

Steve said, "Elissa's found us an assassin. His name is colorful—"

She said, "I met a man named Jack Frost on the grounds at Chadwyck."

"Assassins rarely give their names," said Jay dryly.

"Maybe it's false," she admitted. "But I saw him later in Miami. Now he's here at this hotel. I took his picture and I got his room number. I think the Secret Service ought to check him."

Jay gave her an exasperated look. "Steve, we have a full program tonight. Can we drop this if I have them check him?"

"I told her we can't set the Secret Service—"

"Get down!" Jay shouted.

Before she could move, he lunged toward Steve, shoving her to the floor and carrying Steve forward with him to shelter behind the bed.

"Keep your head down!" he ordered.

As she obeyed, she had a sense of violent movement.

Jay hurled a heavy object that crashed against the wall near the window. For a few moments they lay in silence.

Then Jay said to her: "Stay there."

Cautiously, he looked over the bed, rose, and moved toward the window. After a moment Steve got up and joined him.

"A man was on the ledge," Jay said.

"Where did he go?"

"Maybe the lamp startled him. Stand back," Jay said and opened the window. He leaned out, looked to the right, to the left. Then he looked down. He made a curious sound between surprise and satisfaction.

Elissa got up slowly and joined them. Both men were silent. She looked down and made out a crowd gathering in the dusk below them. "Did he have a gun?"

"All I saw was the silhouette. And I moved," said Jay.

"Amen. And thanks." Steve turned to Elissa. "I gave you a hard time. I'm sorry."

She nodded. She wished she could leave it at that, but she knew now she had to speak. She said in a burst: "But that's not the way it's going to happen! You'll be shot in the secret suite in the museum." She hurried to finish before he stopped her. "I saw it, Steve, just like it was really happening. You were lying on the bed. Your face—" She faltered.

"Gentle Jesus," Jay said in tones of wondering contempt.

"But it was dark so I can't be sure if it really was the museum. It might be any dark bedroom."

At the scorn on Jay's face she stopped.

Steve's voice held regret. "I can't take any more psychic alarms, Elissa. Right now I'll have to talk to the cops. And after that I've got the night's schedule."

She understood that he wasn't going to listen.

"You're going back to the keys."

She nodded unhappily. He didn't trust her near the police. He had covered her warning to the Bomb Squad, but that was in New York, where he was Governor. In California he couldn't chance her.

"Just till things settle down," he said.

She nodded again, not believing the promise.

"Better pack now, hon." And to Jay: "Call the airline for her reservation."

She stared at him in despair. Then she turned and silently left.

Chapter 13

CAMERON ASSASSIN FAILS:
FALLS TO DEATH

SAN FRANCISCO (UPI)—An assassination attempt on the life of Steve Cameron, Governor of New York and Democratic presidential candidate, failed today as his alleged assassin, Jack Frost, 29, a New York City bartender, slipped and plunged to his death while attempting to shoot Cameron through the window of his suite in a San Francisco hotel.

A loaded .32 caliber Clarke "Saturday Night Special" was found near the body.

The alleged assassin, who was registered in the same hotel under the name Walter Van Allen, was also carrying a New York driver's license and an American Express credit card in the name of Van Allen. However, he was identified by his fingerprints with the Bartenders' Union as Jack Frost of New York City.

Mr. Van Allen is being sought for questioning. . . .

As Sam Blake read the story aloud, Delia and Elissa were drinking Cuban coffee on the houseboat sun deck.

Sam lowered the Key West *Citizen* and looked across to Elissa. "He slipped when Dolan threw the lamp at him?"

She nodded then bent to stroke Sam's new dog, Lady. After a sharp look Sam didn't press her with other questions. In a moment her eyes caught on a page from the Miami *Herald* which Sam had scattered beneath the breakfast table. Still upside down while she petted Lady, she began to read:

DOUBLE LIFE OF A KILLER

By Paula Fraser

New York

The tidy clean apartment over the Eighth Avenue pawnshop occupied by the quiet man in his late twenties was being studied today by investigative agents searching for a key to the enigma of his life and death.

A portrait of the man he had tried to kill hung in his bedroom. It was inscribed "To Jack Frost from his friend Steve Cameron." Handwriting experts said it was not written by Cameron.

The bedroom closet contained markedly different sets of wardrobes. One set was mod and flashy. The other was in the style of a conservative country gentleman. Hidden in the closet, agents found a little 9mm Luger.

Jack Frost, whom neighbors described as quiet and courteous, was portrayed by customers at the bar where he worked as open and friendly. Thomas Barton, screenwriter and playwright, said that Jack Frost had been "an intelligent student of the world around him." Manicurist Christine Gillett called him "a sweet guy." He had worked for Cherry's Bar near Central Park for three years. His employer said he had never taken time off until this week. . . .

There was a picture of Jack Frost taken from his bartender's permit and another of the street outside the Fairmont with an arrow pointed to his tarpaulin-covered body.

Elissa studied both pictures. Then she looked across the page to another story.

GRIEF FOR A QUIET COUNTRY BOY

By Cy Stafford

Ossipee, N.H.

"If only he hadn't gone to live in the city," the 84 year old grandmother mourns, tears running down her wrinkled cheeks. Jack Frost, her only grandson, left his small rural town in New Hampshire three years ago to seek his fortune in New York. Now his body lies in the morgue in San Francisco, following an alleged assassination attempt on Steve Cameron, New York Governor and a candidate in the Democratic primaries.

Mrs. Gerald brought him up after his divorced mother, Trudy Frost, abandoned him as an infant. Mrs. Gerald hasn't heard from her daughter since that day twenty-eight years ago. For Jack's father, a one-time ballplayer, it is an even longer silence.

"Jackie was a good boy," she says, twisting her work-gnarled hands in her lap. "He worked hard here on the farm. He went to our church every Sunday. He didn't smoke or drink. He took the White Ribbon pledge when he was twelve. I don't know how he came to be a bartender."

After high school he clerked at the local grocery store for a while. But mostly Jack Frost took odd jobs

—handyman, picking apples, selling firewood, pumping gas at a gas station. He was restless and never stayed with a job long. Then, "He got it in his mind he had to see the big city. He saved up for a suit and took the Greyhound bus to New York. He didn't write regular but he never forgot my birthday or Christmas. He sent the money for this television set," she says sadly.

Now she sits before the television set watching the news accounts of how her grandson tried to kill the New York Governor. "I don't believe it," she says. "He never bothered none with politics." Her old dog watches her, trying to understand why she weeps.

"He was quiet, not much of a student but always polite," Mr. Pomeroy, his English teacher, says at the high school in Wolfeboro. "He got on best with older people."

The Zambresky family, however, remembers him differently. They say he was violent when he was angry.

Mrs. Zambresky, a worn, graying mother, remembers. Jack and her boy, Pete, became friends in high school. "They ran around together, went fishing for pike and pickerel, quail hunting, like that. Then they fought over something. Jack said Pete took his hunting knife, some little thing. But Jack went crazy. He nearly killed Pete with a tire iron."

Pete smiles from his wheelchair. He is a thin young man in an old bathrobe. "I marked him up good with a rock though."

His mother hushes him. "Pete fell but Jack kept on hitting. He smashed the back of his head. Pete was in the hospital for months. He still can't move his legs. He spends his time in the wheelchair."

Yes, Pete Zambresky and his mother also remember Jack Frost, the quiet boy from the country. . . .

* * *

Delia set down her coffee mug and got up from the table. "I guess I'd better go do my errands. Groceries, and I'm out of books. I'll stop by the library. Anyone want to come?"

"I can't," Sam said with an air of virtue. "I'm working on my last chapter."

"Hey, daddy, not really!" said Elissa. She'd given up waiting for the announcement years earlier.

"Isn't that *fine?*" As Delia's thin countenance lighted, she seemed almost beautiful. The yearning brown eyes and her long, graceful nose were beautiful. It occurred to Elissa that Delia reminded her of the fairy tale deer who was really a princess under the enchantment of an evil magician. Who had been the magician? Delia's professor father back in Indiana? And had Sam, unlikely prince, broken the spell? It was a curious idea, she thought, to have about your father. Observed from outside, their pairing had seemed almost ridiculous—an aging spinster's love for a skinny, battered ex-drunk—especially strange to Elissa, who had lived with Sam all her life and to whom Sam was just a father, a sometimes loved, occasionally pitied, often maddening presence, whose two books had been published so long ago they were nearly forgotten, and whose third unfinished book had come to seem a hopeless delusion. Yet Delia, with new faith, had awaited a masterpiece. And like a miracle, the book was nearly done. She felt a new respect for Delia.

"It's a great book, wait and see," Delia told her.

"She ought to know. Every time I change a line, she retypes it," said Sam lightly, and Elissa sensed profound emotion cloaked by the lightness. For an instant she wished she could live in the world they had so painstakingly put together. It was like being flung into space being exiled from Steve, and she was lonely for the first time in her life.

When Delia left, Sam hung over the houseboat railing

watching her start the old Volks with the fenders dented
by years of his drinking. "See if they have cherries! And
I need more murder mysteries from the library!" And as
Delia executed an old-time radio engineer's circling
gesture of understanding, he shouted, "Bring me a
surprise!"

"What kind of a surprise?" asked Elissa.

"Ice cream or eclairs, something sweet, she'll know
what."

Elissa shook her head, smiling. It was growing harder
to remember the Sam who had existed before Delia, the
Sam who reeled down back alleys tracked by the faithful
dog, Black Bart, the Sam of hospital emergency rooms and
nights spent in the lockup.

"Sure you don't want to go with Delia? It's going to be
a hot day for biking," he said in a more fatherly manner.

"Thought I might take the skiff out. Okay?"

"Sure. You'll need gas. Charge it," he said, nodding
toward the yacht club gas pumps.

"Where's my gear?"

"In your bunkroom." When she'd arrived on the first
plane from Miami that morning, Delia had already trans-
formed Sam's office back into her bunkroom. "The Cuban
handline's in the fishbox. They'll give you bait, too, at the
gas pumps."

She went to her bunkroom and returned with a faded
shirt over her bikini. Over her shoulder she carried an
old fishnet gear bag with her mask, snorkel, and flippers.
A battered straw hat sat on her head. She went to the
galley and tossed some oranges into the gear bag.

"Want a sandwich?" Sam asked. "Delia always keeps
cheese in the icebox." As she shook her head, he and Lady
followed her downstairs.

At the stern of the houseboat, as she dropped her gear
into the skiff, she was conscious of Sam's gaze upon her.

"What really happened in San Francisco?" he asked.

She turned and was caught by the concern in his lined face. "A man tried to kill Steve, like they said in the papers."

"What brought you home then?"

She hesitated.

"It's only two days before the California primary. They must be busy. Strange time for a vacation," he said. "What's wrong, toots? I'm a tough old bird. I've seen a lot of trouble. Most of it of my own making, of course, but still, there's nothing shocking you can tell me."

"All right," she said slowly. "Remember when I phoned and said mother was psychic?"

He looked surprised and disappointed. "That's what you get for listening to Valdez. She was always cuckoo about the supernatural."

"But what if she really was psychic?" And before he could answer, "What if those insects trying to get in her brain were telepathic images of Elinor's brain cancer?"

"That's impossible!" he snorted.

"Professor Young doesn't think so. He says a lot of psychics end up in mental hospitals. A boy he's working with who's telepathic came out of Rockland."

"Veronica hallucinated," he interrupted. "She was unstable and LSD tipped her over into psychosis!" And as Elissa's gaze slipped away in disagreement, "Who the hell is this professor?"

"His name is Don Young. He has a psi lab and he's been testing me for precognition. I saw the Rockefeller Center bombing before it happened. I heard a rape and murder. And I saw Steve—assassinated."

"He's alive for God's sake!"

"I'm afraid he's going to be shot to death."

Sam took a grip on himself and, she guessed, decided to reason inside her delusion. "Okay, say it's all true, Elissa. Maybe you *can* see the future. What if what you saw in San Francisco was the attempt? It failed and now it's over. So you can stop worrying."

"I saw him *dead*, daddy! There was blood—and a tooth —he was murdered. The trouble is, my seeing . . . things . . . makes him nervous. He's not sure if I'm psychic or crazy. He sent me home. Out of his life."

There was a silence. Then he sighed. "Out of his life. That means you've fallen for him."

She nodded.

"Too old for you, of course. Too much glamour, too much money, too much power." He paused. "I can't quite see you in the White House either."

She smiled wryly. "Well, you asked."

"So I did. I got puffed up and important and figured I could help you. But there's not much help for love. Except time."

"I know." She turned and stepped into the skiff, her pale hair swinging. As she started up, Lady barked sharply.

"Take her with you. She fishes," Sam called over the noise of the motor.

"What does that mean?"

"You'll see," Sam shouted and Lady leaped in beside her. Suddenly Sam called again, "This professor—he says you really saw that bombing?"

"He got it on tape. Hours before it happened."

Sam considered with an air of reluctance. "Okay. It's hard, but I guess I'll have to accept it."

"Thanks, Daddy. It's tough, people thinking that you're crazy."

"And if we could still help your mother—get her out, even bring her down here—"

"It's too late. They gave her a lobotomy."

His face drained. "But nobody asked me! I had to sign before they could do that!"

"She was using her maiden name and I guess Claudia didn't tell them she was married."

He stared at her, speechless.

She called, "I'm sorry, Daddy." She hadn't intended to tell him, and certainly not this way, shouting above a boat motor. She almost went back to try to comfort him, then she decided that Sam's way had always been to work through a blow by himself.

He was still motionless when she headed for the gas dock.

The skiff was in better shape than she remembered; better, in fact, than she had ever seen it. It had been cleaned, scrubbed, even recently painted, she supposed by Delia.

But as she slipped away from the gas pumps and headed out the bight past the old naval station, her thoughts returned to Veronica as to a wound that wouldn't heal over.

There had been so little memory or understanding in the ruined, once lovely features, that she couldn't bring herself to face another actual visit. Instead, she had gone back to leave a few things for Veronica's present comfort— warm slippers, a new bathrobe, a basket of fruit. And as she turned from the nurses' office outside the .waiting room, she had run into Valdez.

Valdez looked shockingly older. Her skin had a gray pallor and the brilliant black eyes were dulled and bitter.

"Did you see mother?" Elissa asked.

"I've been coming since you told me where they put her."

"She doesn't know who I am. And I haven't been able to make myself visit."

"Don't," Valdez advised. "You're too young to cope with that kind of senseless butchery. I'm old and I'm used to hating. But hate is dangerous. It can be fatal if you haven't built up a tolerance."

At the banked rage in her voice, Elissa fell into step with her in silence. Silently, they rode down in the elevator, left the pavilion, and caught the bus for Manhattan as it was leaving.

Then as they rode across the East River, Valdez muttered in what sounded like a foreign language.

"What?" Elissa asked, trying to mask her alarm. Valdez was older than she looked; perhaps she was reverting to the Spanish of her childhood. And yet it didn't sound like the usual Key West Cuban Spanish.

"Procrustes," Valdez repeated. "Don't you know your Greek myths?"

"I'm afraid not."

"And they tax us for what they call education," Valdez grumbled. "Procrustes tied his visitors to a bed, then lopped off the parts that didn't fit. Society is the bed of Procrustes. If you're different, they lop off the bits that don't fit. Elinor was a poet, a free spirit, and was different. I watched two men try to change her into an ordinary woman. By the time they finished, she was a crazy old woman. And Veronica was different. You see what happened." She paused. "I hope to God you're not different."

"I'm afraid I'm like mother. I . . . see things," Elissa said with misgiving.

Valdez glanced at her but Elissa didn't try to explain and Valdez didn't question her further. They lapsed back into silence for the rest of the ride.

When they got off the bus at 125th Street, Valdez asked, "Can I give you a lift? I'm working up a show at a gallery on East Seventy-second."

"No, I have to go to the Village. I'll take the subway."

Suddenly Valdez burned through the gray mask of her aging. Her black eyes flamed and she clawed her gray hair with strong fingers. "Be careful," she ordered vehemently. "Don't tell them anything! Nothing threatens them like the inexplicable. If they can't pigeonhole you, they'll lock you up or kill you!"

And before Elissa could speak again, she hailed a passing taxi and was gone.

With effort Elissa brought herself back to the present, deliberately focused on running the skiff, watching for markers to Man Key, and reading the blue waters that had always healed her.

It was a day of perfections: The Gulf was the color of cornflowers, glassed off and clear to the bottom so that she seemed to be moving over air. A leopard ray fled before her. Then Lady barked and she turned toward the shining arcs of porpoises. The tightness in her shoulders loosened. She shook back her pale hair and gazed up at the summer clouds. Soon she made out the familiar white curve of the mangrove-fringed beach.

Lady fished. There was no doubt about it. She stood in the clear water that lapped Man Key, her neck arched, shivering with hunter's passion, nose pointed like a speartip at the small, translucent fish. Then she leaped, burying her muzzle in the water.

Elissa tried to decide if Lady really caught and swallowed the fish. If she did, there was no moment of triumph, no relaxing of the hunt's compulsion. At once her pepper-and-salt flanks tautened, her neck bowed. The black nose pointed again with fatal intention. When Elissa flung water toward her, Lady let out a joyful bark. Next moment, she was fixed on the darting fish.

Elissa lay back for a while in the shallow water. The June sun moving toward its zenith glazed the cove's surface so that every so often she shut her eyes against it and gave herself up to feeling the cool current moving across her body.

At last she sat up and peeled an orange. She ate with slow attention, then lay back again and watched the floating orange peel. Soon she would rise and look for the rickety tree house someone had built long ago beyond the beach. She would search for the single old tree farther back on the key that sheltered long grass and wild lilies.

But she kept extending the lazy wholeness of the present, trying to remember the way she'd been before she'd met Steve, when she had been a creature complete in herself, autonomous, serene, and free.

The tree house was gone, fallen and disassembled for casual cookouts, but the old tree still stood and she fell asleep in the long grasses with Lady snoozing beside her.

When she woke, the glare that burned in the air had softened and the shade beneath the tree had extended. But for a bit more, she lay watching three frigate birds riding the thermals. A flight of ibis wheeled above her in formation, and she heard the low-pitched call of doves behind in the mangroves. It was the way she had spent the best hours of her childhood—first with Sam, and then as Sam had been sucked deeper into his addictions, she had learned to run the skiff and come out by herself. Her past was here, on this and sister islands, and for a while she tried to reach that younger Elissa who'd been alone but part of a whole, too, unthinkingly linked to the flight of birds, the piling clouds, the ballyhoos skimming the surface of the water. That Elissa had spent entire afternoons by herself with contentment.

But she was only able to picture, not touch or reach into that Elissa. She was alone but it was unsatisfying. There was a sense of loss now, a vacuum within her, a sick misery at losing Steve.

Falling in love was an illness, she decided, painful and demoralizing. Her misery was self-inflicted. He had not asked her to fall in love with him.

It hadn't been like that when she had towed him back to Tarpon Island, when she had first met the tribe of Camerons, nor in the years Steve had been away, had married, had his children. Watching the slowly wheeling frigate birds, she tried to decide when her feelings had darkened, when the joy had begun to be painful, when she had first felt jealousy and unreasoning anger. But she couldn't pinpoint a moment. Letting it go, she was filled with a need to return to childhood's clarity. Simultaneously she was assaulted by the memory of Steve's features, his expressions, his voice's timbre. Distracted by the conflict, she sent out an anguished plea to Something—if there was Something—to heal her of loving and set her free.

By late afternoon she had caught two snappers with her Cuban handline and was diving the coral heads off Man Key.

While Lady poked her nose over the skiff's side and watched her, she kicked her flippers and moved slowly down a stand of staghorn coral as a school of snapper moved off and an angel fish took shelter behind a sea fan. A lobster scooted backwards. A little blue hamlet dipped inside an empty conch shell. Only the black-and-yellow sergeant majors kept swimming about her. And a barracuda hung motionless above.

When she reached the bottom, she saw a sand dollar. She put her hand out to touch it when she sighted the moray.

Its unblinking snake's head regarded her from a crevice in the coral. Surprised, she sculled backwards.

As she kicked herself to the surface and cleared her snorkel, she had a sense of having been there before, of descending past that stand of staghorn in a swirl of sergeant majors, of seeing that particular blue hamlet. Even the moray peering out the fissure in the coral . . . As she teased her memory, a prickling began in the pit of her stomach, a coldness and a dark sense of rapidly approaching danger.

It was so strong that she turned in a slow circle, searching the coral heads for some lurking creature considering her as prey, perhaps a tiger shark or hammerhead. But she saw nothing; she wasn't being menaced. "Stop!" she told herself in annoyance. Then the moray touched her mind again. And suddenly she remembered.

It had been one of her pictures while Don was testing her at the psi lab, the day she'd seen Billy's attack of grand mal and the Rockefeller Center bombing. But what had the picture been precisely? The stand of staghorn coral, the blue hamlet, the school of sergeant majors, the moray glaring out of its hole, and like a dark stain, the sense of oncoming danger.

She grabbed the skiff's prop to support herself and hung, thinking. Maybe it had been a precognition averted, like the case of the chandelier above the baby's crib. Perhaps the moray had been about to attack her. If she'd been an inch nearer when she reached for the sand dollar, the snake's head might have flashed from its crevice and the sharp teeth fastened on her arm or leg. It was the greatest danger in the keys' waters. A strong man couldn't pull free from a moray without a knife to cut off its head or his own arm. She would have fought to hold her breath till her air was exhausted, then despite herself, she would have gasped in salt water, choked, gasped in more, at last become unconscious, and drowned. The eel would have shared her with the barracuda, crabs, and lobster in the long night while Lady kept vigil in the little skiff. Till the first morning fisherman saw the dog and empty boat and came closer to investigate.

She shivered, dove and pulled the anchor, dropped it over the bow, and hauled herself in to safety.

It was nearly sunset when she surfaced. As she toweled off, she watched the waters blackening, the red sun slipping toward the horizon, and the edges of the clouds touched with luminescence. When she was a child, Coconut Charley had told her that if she saw a green flash as the sun set, she'd have a stroke of good fortune. It wasn't true, of course, but she always thought of it at sunset, and this evening, too, she lingered till the last of the red ball sank, flashless, into the ocean.

Then she heard the distant throb of an engine. She looked for a plane but there was no plane. It was a boat moving beneath the half moon on the southern horizon. Soon she saw the boat itself, a speck at first, then slightly larger, till in the dimming air, she made out a white wake. It was running fast; the driver must know the local waters.

When its running lights flashed on, she stood holding her damp towel around her, trying to identify it, but it wasn't a boat she recognized. It was fairly big, perhaps an Excalibur, which meant twin 200s or 225s. A lovely boat, fast and expensive.

As it came closer, she stared through the twilight trying to make out the outline of the lone man standing at the wheel. He was tall, rangy, well muscled—

He put up an arm and waved to her.

"Hey," she whispered. It was Steve.

He made his approach fast, cut his motor, and drifted to her, grabbing the skiff's side to hold off the Excalibur. As Lady barked, she hushed her.

"What are you doing here?" she asked.

"I had a free night so I dropped Bob in town till tomorrow morning." Bob was the pilot on his Lear jet, so they must have flown directly in from San Francisco. He'd come to see her rather than gone to Chadwyck or to Albany. Pleasure filled her.

"Where's the Secret Service?"

He grinned. "Gave them the slip. Used my famous hidden ball play."

She smiled, remembering her birthday night at the Nirvana when he'd sent her downstairs while he went to the men's room and out the back way. It wasn't really hard: the Secret Service was there to protect him, not to keep him under surveillance; and he was still not the President, only a primaries candidate. But it made her happy that he'd planned for them to have a private evening.

"How did you find me?"

"I took the car Old Tom leaves at the airport and drove by the houseboat. Your skiff was gone so I got the boat from the point and came looking for you." She remembered the Camerons' boathouse on a key a mile across the water from Tarpon Island; they kept a boat there to get to Tarpon. "How about dinner?" And as she nodded: "I hope you did some serious fishing."

"Not really. All I got was two mangrove snappers."

"Good enough. We'll collect driftwood and cook them on the beach."

"Does your boat draw too much water for Man Key?"

He considered the flats that surrounded the cove. "It's pretty shallow." Then he reached down and threw out his anchor. "We'll use the skiff to run in."

He tossed her a line and she asked, "What's this for?"

"Do you think I'd come this far and not have a swim? Watch for big fish." He peeled down to his trunks and dove in.

She tied his line to her railing and climbed aboard his boat with curiosity. It was her first time in an Excalibur and it was like moving from a Piper Cub into a Concorde. She touched the padded upholstery for high speeds in heavy seas, examined the chrome instruments on the dashboard, which made her think of an airplane cockpit. She shook her head in admiration. At last she sat cross-legged on the bow, rewrapping her towel about her and kept track of his fair head in the blackening waters. Clouds scudded across the stars and the quarter moon behind her. A twilight breeze rose and stirred her hair and curled pale tendrils about her temples.

He was a powerful swimmer. For a long time he sported about the two boats, and then hauled himself back into the Excalibur, took her towel, and began drying himself off. His body was pale from the long winter but he looked in shape; his weight was down from the exertion of constant campaigning and he was still firm-muscled from the years of skiing, diving, and handball.

Only his fine-boned profile seemed drawn and almost stern as she watched him in the growing darkness. She began to wonder if he was still troubled by her warnings. She resisted marring the peace of the evening, and yet she suddenly felt she must resolve it, so that everything was smooth again between them.

"I'm sorry I told you what I saw in the museum," she said finally. "I thought it might save your life."

He moved his head in reflex but he didn't answer. Then straightening, he seemed to try to hurdle his dislike. "All right, Elissa. I'll listen. Tell me what you saw in the museum."

"What I already told you. It was as real as if it were happening. You were lying on the bed. You'd been shot."

"I was dead?"

"Your face was—a tooth was embedded in the head-board."

He nodded slowly. "And my murderer?"

"I heard voices but by the time I looked, he was gone."

"That's all it was then. You saw me shot in the museum." His voice was so patient that she felt her hopes shrivel. "Now you've told me," he said reasonably. "Let's forget it."

"But I was right about the bombing."

The face he turned to her was adamant. She was silent.

After a moment he put his arms about her but she had the sense he was still fighting his irritation. She leaned her head against his chest and nuzzled his throat, hoping the touch of him would bring back the early, carefree feeling. But she felt curiously restless, as if something still was missing.

The thought surfaced gently: He did not smell of aftershave. Of course, he'd been swimming, but still a scent would linger. And immediately after, she realized that he never used it.

With her head still pressed to him, she touched the problem as lightly as if she were trying to unsnarl a knot in thread. What had she smelled the night in the museum? Perhaps Jenny was right. Maybe there had been flowers in the darkness of the future. If she could remember what kind, she might pinpoint the season of danger.

She tried to bring back the memory. It was a sharp, spicy scent.

Then her mind returned to the only time she'd seen Cathy. Almost as clearly as if it were still happening, she saw the familiar station wagon on Duval Street. She went into the boutique and at the counter found the lovely young woman with the long chestnut hair, saw her white slacks, her pale pink man's shirt, smelled the bright fragrance of carnations. Carnations.

"Cathy," she said loudly.

She felt the movement in his chest as he looked down. "You said you didn't see her!"

She didn't move, scarcely breathed.

Did he mean that Cathy had been there? But Cathy was dead. She had been dead then. How could she have seen Cathy in the future?

And then she understood. It wasn't the future she had seen in the museum. She had seen the *past*, the way she'd seen it in the draft riots. Because Steve had been sleeping when she'd gone to shower, she had taken for granted that the body on the bed was his. The room was dark; she'd only glanced at the blood, seen the exploded head.

She drew away from him and their glances traded knowledge.

"Who was it?" she asked. "Who was the man on the bed?"

Chapter 14

He was silent, staring out at the ocean as he absorbed the shock of her knowing. Finally he seemed to come to an uneasy acceptance.

"I was looking for Cathy. She'd been staying in town and she'd been drinking. When she was on the loose, she sometimes holed up in the museum. I found her in bed. With a man. He was drunk, too, and we . . . argued. I grabbed the gun from the nightstand. But he went for me. I lost my head and shot him."

"Where was Cathy when I . . . saw it?"

"The sitting room. I took her in there after it happened."

She tried to put herself in his position. The Governor of the state with a drunken wife and a strange man he had shot to death.

"No one ever knew," he told her.

"How did you—" She hesitated, not wanting to ask him what he had done with the body.

But he understood. "I called Jay. He handled it. I told the museum guard Cathy was ill and he drove us to the sanatorium. He knew she was drunk but I had to get him out of the museum. So that Jay could . . . take care of things."

She imagined the cleaning. Jay had gotten rid of the body. Did he have to wrap it to keep the blood from leaking? Did he use a museum crate to smuggle it out? Did he use a dolly? Then a car? And then the river? After that he'd had to clean the bedroom. He'd had to take apart the headboard and destroy the tooth. She began to feel queasy and switched off the picture.

"What about the museum guard? Didn't he wonder about the man who came in with Cathy disappearing?"

"Why would he wonder? He'd figure he left with Jay later, while we were taking Cathy to the sanatorium."

"And nobody looked for him?"

"I don't think he had a family. He didn't have any I.D. He had no wallet with him. So we waited. We read the papers. But nothing turned up." She imagined the days, the weeks of waiting.

"So you don't even know who he was."

He brought his gaze back from the ocean. "His name was Walter Van Allen."

She waited till the name fell into place. "Wasn't that Jack Frost's other name?"

"He used it."

Her silence prodded him into speech.

"Frost was a bartender. Van Allen came into the bar and they struck up a friendship. When Van Allen ran out of money, Frost took him in and let him sleep in his apartment. Then Cathy went on a drunk and wandered into the bar one night. She got talking with Van Allen. When Frost closed up, they all left together. Frost walked them as far as the museum, then he went on. But Van Allen never came home. He disappeared, leaving his clothes, his wallet, all his possessions. So Frost knew something had happened to him."

"He didn't go to the police?"

"No. He was pretty flaky. Maybe he thought they

would suspect him. Maybe he just didn't like the police. Anyway, he started hanging around the museum and made friends with the night watchman. He found out from him who Cathy was. But it took him a while—by then she'd killed herself."

"Was it because of what happened?"

"She never knew. She was in a blackout that night. When she came to, she was in the sanatorium."

"But weren't you worried? What if she'd remembered and told the doctors?"

"She'd been there before. They wouldn't have believed her. They'd have thought it was just her usual nightmares. Besides, they gave her electric shock. It wipes out recent memory."

She was quiet, wondering if Steve had agreed to the shock because it wiped out memory. Afterward, in despair, had Cathy slashed her throat? She felt sick as she thought of Veronica's lobotomy. She forced herself to wipe out the image, but it dissolved into Jack Frost's face, became Cathy again, a gallery of the odd, the damned, the misunderstood.

"I wonder why he came to San Francisco."

He smiled wryly. "He wanted to be my friend."

She looked up in incomprehension.

"Apparently he hung around Chadwyck hoping to run into me. Maybe Miami, too. Finally he wrote to me in Albany. But he was so careful, my secretary thought it was just another crank letter. We get so many of them, we have a form we send. So he came to San Francisco and left a note in my hotel box. It said he'd seen Cathy and Van Allen going into the museum that night. He told what he'd put together from the guard, too—how Jay arrived and the guard left with me to drive Cathy to the sanatorium. And of course, Van Allen's disappearance. It might not have stood up in court but the newspapers would have had a field day. It would have ruined me."

"But why did he try—" She stopped, struck by the

thought that maybe Jack Frost hadn't tried to kill him. She hadn't actually seen Frost on the ledge. Jay had only said he'd been there. Jay, who had got rid of Van Allen's body. And Jay had just the moment before walked into Steve's hotel suite. He might have come from Jack's room on the floor above.

"Jay killed him! He went to see him and pushed him out the window. When Jay said he was on the ledge, he was already dead!"

His silence was his admission.

"But why did Jay say that Jack Frost was trying to kill you?"

"He didn't intend to. He'd bought a Saturday Night Special and gone to silence him. It would have looked like he'd killed himself. Even when Frost fought back and Jay pushed him out the window, it would have still been just another jumper. He was nobody special. Nobody would have tied him to us. And God knows we didn't want a connection." He paused and then said bitterly, "But you turned up and knew all about him. You'd even seen him before at Chadwyck and in Miami. You knew his name and wanted to call in the Secret Service."

She nodded slowly. With Frost already dead and the crowd gathering below, it must have been an awful moment.

"Jay had to think fast. He threw the lamp and said he'd seen him on the ledge."

"I still don't see what he wanted."

Steve said quickly, "It was a form of blackmail."

"But you said he wanted to be friends!"

"He was flaky. Who could trust him? You have to see that."

She saw that he expected she would understand as Jay did, Jay, who would kill to put Steve in the White House. She had a grotesque picture of a murderous President.

She had felt Steve's pain at finding Cathy betraying him, the sudden struggle, the gun. But she was sickened by the coverup, the disposal of Van Allen's body, and the efficient, detached removal of Jack Frost.

He felt her withdrawal. "You've got to see how it happened. I couldn't undo it. What good would it have done to tell the cops and let the newspapers have an orgy?" And when she kept silent, "If you think about it, you'll understand. It would have meant the presidency."

Some resonance within her told her he spoke an awful truth. He would explain and work on her and use her feeling for him till she understood it.

She didn't frame the words or know where her rebellion headed. "I'm going home now."

"Don't take a high moral line with me, Elissa!" He put a hand on her arm and she quickly withdrew it. Then, as his face darkened in the moonlight, fright seared her. She whirled and jumped over the side of the Excalibur into the skiff. He reached toward her and desperately she began untying the line that held the Excalibur to the skiff's railing. As she freed the skiff, he lunged toward her in the darkness like a darker shadow. She heard frantic barking. Then something struck her.

When she came to consciousness, she found herself in the water. She felt groggy so that everything seemed to be happening in slow motion. Every movement seemed to take forever, so that she had time to think, This can't be happening.

Then the prow of the Excalibur loomed before her.

She reached out to it but her wet fingers slipped and she went down again. As she resurfaced, she heard the roar of the Excalibur's engines and she cried out at the thought of the two powerful props slicing the water beside her.

I'll be killed! she thought.

In desperation, she lunged upward, caught and clung to the boat's side. Then she saw him, lit by moonlight, leaving the wheel and coming toward her. She was gasping and hauling herself into the boat when he pushed her. As

she fell, she clutched at him, caught his arms, and felt him
lose his balance. Then they were both floundering in the
black water.

Blinded, she shouted, "Steve!" Then her head was
brutally thrust under.

That was when she finally understood. He was going
to drown her.

She tried to pull away but as his hand slipped from her
shoulder, he grabbed her long hair and looped it over his
arm. She lunged upward toward him but he was too strong
for that maneuver, and he held her head down.

She was caught then. She couldn't escape him.

As she held her breath against her last automatic
indrawing, she turned her mind outward toward Somebody—if there was Somebody—and made an anguished
plea for help. Her chest felt as if it were bursting.

She could scarcely believe it when she felt the other
presence. At first she thought it was an effect of her
dwindling consciousness, but then she felt the presence
more clearly. Its force was increasing. In another moment
she caught a familiar feeling-tone. A voice in her mind
said, "Billy."

Later she couldn't catch it with the nets of language.
She felt a sudden calm. And in the calm she withdrew
from the girl struggling in the black water and joined her
strength with the arriving strength. They merged, locked
together, and grew stronger. Then their joint will grew
one-pointed.

"Now!" She felt the order and they moved in mental
unison.

They turned toward the hand wrapped in her long hair.
As they touched Steve's mind and probed for feeling-
tone, the hand jerked. Then they struck deep and wiped
him clear of consciousness.

The hand relaxed.

"Now!" Billy's voice-feeling ordered.

She kicked and glided upward.

She broke the surface and gasped in air hoarsely. Then she opened her eyes and saw the star-scattered, scudding-cloud sky, and felt the soft warm night on her forehead.

The Excalibur rode at anchor near her. She could hear its motors still running. But the skiff was yards away and moving slowly seaward. She could hear Lady's anguished barking.

She turned then and with long powerful strokes made for her boat. The tide was with her and she was easy in the water as a porpoise. She sliced the dimpled whirlpools of the dark surface, gained on the moving skiff, and reached it. She grabbed the rail and hauled herself to the deck. Then her legs suddenly gave out and she sank down and held onto Lady.

In a few moments her thoughts cleared and she thought of Steve Cameron. If she moved now, it still might be possible to save him. She could start up the skiff and return to the Excalibur. If she dove, she might be able to find him. With luck she might get him into the boat and start resuscitation.

She pictured him down among the coral heads, the piercing Cameron eyes staring at the dark water, the brilliant smile only a rictus, the athlete's chest laboring for air but filling with water, and she felt a pull so strong she was almost unable to resist it.

She didn't remember that he had tried to drown her. Instead she remembered the eager young man she had towed long ago to Tarpon Island, and then the powerful man who had solved all her problems in a Manhattan police station. He still held her.

It was four minutes—five—by now too long for his brain to be without oxygen. The man she had loved was gone already. She could not bring him back to live with a ruined brain. She locked her hands about her ankles and, putting her head on her knees, she waited, keeping vigil.

"Billy," the voice whispered in her mind. She lifted her head. "Okay? Okay?" the voice asked.

She looked at the sky, the stars, the lopsided moon, and turned her mind outward. "I'm here. I'm here," she cried silently.

She felt a question and then he transmitted the feeling-tone of Steve Cameron.

"Dead." She felt a question and she tried to send a picture of a boat, the blow on the head, her fall into the water. But it was too complex. She couldn't hold it all together.

As if a radio band had snapped on, she heard the murmur of new voices. She couldn't make out what they said, and though they sounded gentle, they were strange and suddenly she was frightened.

But her sense of Billy came again. "Okay. You. Us. Others."

The voices rose like a breeze rustling in the mangroves. Others. Other psis. Other telepaths. From the psi lab? From the Premonitions Bureau?

"No hurt," the sense came. And she realized the real, the only danger—Billy put in Rockland State for picking up his brother's thoughts, Veronica shuffling through her life in paper slippers, she herself nearly drowned because she'd seen too much.

As she sat in the little skiff with her hair clinging wetly about her shoulders, its chrysalis moisture gave her the look of a newly unfurling creature. A cloud raced across the quarter moon and her hair shone like phosphorescence.

When the voices came again, she raised her face to the warm softness of the night, her lips parting, as she greeted them.